SAD EYES

BOOK ONE   1912 TO 1939

DAN PERKINS

Daniel 12/7/25

To Bill Enjoy

Jan-Carol Publishing, Inc

"every story needs a book"

Also by Dan Perkins

The Brotherhood of the Red Nile, A Terrorist Perspective

The Brotherhood of the Red Nile, America Rebuilds

The Brotherhood of the Red Nile, America Responds

Terrorist Gold

Peter, The Little Irish Seal

Why Grammy Can't Remember Me

Timmy and the Little Red Wagon

SAD EYES

BOOK ONE 1912 TO 1939

Sad Eyes
Book 1: 1912 to 1939
Dan Perkins
Published November 2023
Little Creek Books
Imprint of Jan-Carol Publishing, Inc.
All rights reserved
Copyright © 2023 Dan Perkins

ISBN: 978-1-962561-06-8
Library of Congress Control Number: 2023949225

You may contact the publisher:
Jan-Carol Publishing, Inc.
PO Box 701
Johnson City, TN 37605
publisher@jancarolpublishing.com
www.jancarolpublishing.com

This book is dedicated to:

Rear Admiral Scott Logan, My Dear Friend

He passed away before this book was finished.

He was always a sucker for a good story.

Gerri Perkins, My Wife and Editor

We wrote a great story because of her dedication and patience.

She taught me how the novel needed to be written.

From the Author

I have been called a master storyteller. *Sad Eyes* is my first attempt at writing a historical romance.

I was very excited to write about Mary Ellen Murphy. I loved the commitment she had to her values, and all the things she accomplished. It was remarkable to write about the setting leading up to and including the Second World War and encompassing The Greatest Generation.

I'm told that the "Life Lessons Learned" at the end of each chapter enriches the story, and I hope you agree. This is such a rich story that I had to split the manuscript into two books, covering two time frames. The first book starts in 1912, and the second book begins in 1939 and ends in 1951.

It took over two years after finishing the book to get it published. The previous publisher let me down, but I'm enjoying my new publisher, Janie C. Jessee with Jan-Carol Publishing, Inc. She calls me one of her best unknown authors. We hope you like the first book!

Prologue

This is the story of the most extended honeymoon in history. It is my story. It is also a story that is unfinished.

My name is Mary Ellen Murphy, and I was 39 when I started to write *Sad Eyes* in 1951. I wrote it to preserve my memory of the events that impacted me during the first 39 years of my life.

Between my sophomore and junior years of high school, I decided to be a nurse. I realized my dream, and what an adventure it's been. It has had its ups and downs, but I would not change a thing. I hope you enjoy my story.

Mary Ellen Murphy
September 1, 1951

The Nurse's Pledge:

"I solemnly pledge myself before God and in the presence of this assembly: to pass my life in purity and to practice my profession faithfully. I will abstain from whatever is deleterious and mischievous and will not take or knowingly administer any harmful drug. I will do all in my power to maintain and elevate the standard of my profession. I will confidently hold all personal matters committed to my keeping and all family affairs coming to my knowledge in the practice of my calling. With loyalty, will I endeavor to aid the physician in his work and devote myself to the welfare of those committed to my care?"

CHAPTER 1:

I Was Born to Do Something

My name is Mary Ellen Murphy, and I am a red-haired, green-eyed Irish lass born on September 5, 1912, before the First World War broke out on July 28, 1914. I am the second child of three born to James and Margaret Murphy. My older sister is named Kelly, and my younger brother is Patrick. My parents are second-generation Irish from County Cork, Ireland. We belong to Saint Mary's Catholic Church on East Fourth and Parker Street in Waterloo, Iowa. It is a typical small town of about 25,000 people.

My father works at a machine shop, and my mother is a seamstress in a dressmaker's shop in downtown Waterloo. When I was little, my mom worked from home to be with me and my brother and sister. Now that we are older, she goes to work at the shop downtown. My brother, sister and I leave for school while our parents go to work. At a very early age, I think about 12, I realize that I don't want to do what many young people do in Waterloo. I don't want to go through high school, get married, have many children, and stay in Waterloo for the rest of my life. It may work for others, but it is not for me.

I became interested in science in my freshman year at Our Lady of Victory High School. I don't think that I would like to be a doctor, but

I do think seriously from time to time about becoming a nurse. I don't know why being a nurse is so attractive. The only nurse I ever met was in our family doctor's office. I have never, at least as far as I can remember, been in a hospital. I'm an avid reader; the library is like my second home. Whenever I don't know something, I go to the library and look it up.

Early in my first year, I start looking for books on nurses to check out on one of my regular visits to the library. Unfortunately, my library does not have many books about nursing. I read stories about the nurses who served in the Civil War, and I am interested in two women who changed the nursing profession, Clara Barton and Dorothea Dix.

I am intrigued with Barton because she was determined to implement what she believed was the best way to treat injured soldiers. Dorothea Dix was chosen by Abraham Lincoln as the first superintendent of U.S. Army nurses in 1861. She set the tone of what a nurse should be. They must be between 35 and 50 years of age, in good health, of high moral standards, not too attractive, and lastly, be willing to dress plainly.

I'm glad I didn't live back then, because I am not 35. I am in good health and believe I have a solid moral foundation. I am not boastful, but many people, including boys, think I am attractive. Last of all, I do not dress plainly. I like to wear comfortable clothes but simultaneously demonstrate that I am what some would call "a full-blown woman." Sometimes I do want to tease the boys in town. Someday, I will find the right man, fall in love, get married, have a few children, and grow old with my man, but not in Waterloo.

I still find it hard to believe that women were supposed to work with doctors during the Civil War, assisting them in everything without formal training. It must have been challenging to work for a doctor. You must have had to be a fast learner. I am a quick learner and hope to do well in nursing school in Chicago. I want to attend school in a big city, and Chicago is perfect, even though I have never been there. I found a book in the public library on the history of nurses in America where I learned that it wasn't until 1872 that the New England Hospital for Women and Children opened the first school for nurses. The curriculum was one year in length. Can you believe that? I did three years in my diploma program at St. James Hospital in Chicago.

At the end of my sophomore year of high school, it has been less than 60 years from the formation of the first school of nursing and about 65 years from the end of the Civil War. During the summer of 1929, before my junior year of high school, I tell my mom and dad that I want to be a nurse and go to St. James Hospital Nursing School in Chicago. My mother is the first to speak. My father sits and listens. Mom thinks it is significant that I want to attend nursing school but wonders why I must go to Chicago, and *what is wrong with St. Ambrose in Iowa?* She says it is closer, and I can still be with my family. I can see my father nodding in agreement with what my mom says. I begin to realize this is going to be a tough sell.

I tell my mom there is nothing wrong with St. Ambrose's, but I want to see the big city and do things that I probably never would be able to do if I stayed in Waterloo. I need to grow, and I think going to nursing school and being in Chicago will make me a better nurse. I have some brochures from St. Ambrose and some from St. James in Chicago that I want them to look at, and then we can talk again. My father and mother agree to look at the brochures, and then we will speak again. They tell me how proud they are of me for wanting to do such important work with my life.

Life Lessons Learned:

Some people are blessed because they know what they want to do with their lives and seek it out. They build a plan for accomplishing their goals while still a teenager. It's essential to have your parents' support.

A person who knows what they want to do becomes motivated and has a central focus on what will be necessary to succeed. The most challenging thing for parents is to allow children to decide what they will do with their lives. Sometimes, parents can see whether their child can be successful. On the other hand, children are only sometimes singularly focused; often, children float from one thing to another and, unfortunately, never conclude.

One thing my parents never told me, and I never told my children, was that I couldn't do some things. It was sometimes painful, but it was always important as I got older to take responsibility for my decisions and outcomes, good or bad.

CHAPTER 2:

The Beginnings

My parents' house is at 1575 Myrtle Ave., Waterloo, Iowa. My sister, three years older than me, and my younger brother, three years younger than me, were all born at home. In those days, very few babies were born in hospitals. When my brother Patrick was born, I thought it natural that my newborn brother was nursing at the same breast I did until recently.

The day I am born, I don't know it, but the First World War is two years away, nor do I know how familiar I will become with war. In 1917, there is no radio for entertainment. We must make our entertainment. Sometimes, if we have the money, we go to the picture show and sit and watch a silent movie. It is fantastic to see those people move on the screen. I laugh a lot and eat much popcorn.

We spend much time playing outside in our yard and the woods at Myrtle Ave.'s end. A small lake fed by a stream is in the woods. We swim there in the summer, fish in it most of the year, and skate on the ice in the winter. Once or twice, I try ice fishing, but I need to get warmer to continue. I have always preferred the cold. I would run home and beg my mom for hot cocoa to warm me up. All of us have bikes, so we are constantly riding them everywhere. We have simple toys. My sister has a Flossy baby doll that says, "Mama," and moves its eyes. Because she is a dressmaker, Mom makes clothes for Flossy out of fabric scraps she brings home from the store. Her dresses are more elegant than any doll clothes you can buy in the store or from the Sears and Roebuck catalog.

While petite, I have a teddy bear I take everywhere. I always take Teddy to bed with me. My sister and I play checkers with our neighbors on the street. We ride our bikes to school. Sometimes we have races to see who gets home the fastest.

Our bedrooms are on the second floor. We have three bedrooms. One room is for my parents. My sister Kelly and I share the next one, and the third room is for Patrick. My sister and I share a bed with a beige chenille coverlet. The house is heated, such as it is, by a coal furnace. The heat rarely makes it to our bedrooms. We have registers on the floor of each room because the heat rises, and the theory is that the heat from the first floor would come up the stairs and through the registers. At least, that is the theory. The reality is different. Our rooms are cold and freezing in the heart of winter. I wait as long as possible to go to bed because I know the outhouse and my bedroom are freezing. I never move faster than I do going from the outhouse to my bedroom on a cold winter night in January.

The living room has a fireplace. My mom uses a wood stove to cook on, which best heats the kitchen. I often wonder why my parents' room is above the kitchen stove. Then, I figure out that the heat from the kitchen goes up into their bedroom. The furnace has a fire from early morning to late at night all year round. I spend many a winter's night with my brother and sister doing my homework or reading at the table in the kitchen and watching my mother make bread and sweets on that table. It has what they call an oilcloth on it. It is heavy-duty and easy to clean. My mom keeps a 3-gallon pot of water on the stove during the winter night. She keeps it just off the plate of the furnace so that the water won't boil, just steam. Each of us has a large, dark red, hot water bottle we fill just before bed to take the chill off the bed and keep us warm. On cold nights, I get up, put on my heavy chenille robe, hurry to the kitchen, and refill my bottle.

My mother has two oilcloth covers for the table. One is used for preparing food, and the other is for eating. The one for eating has a bright flower pattern to make the dinner table look fancy. Our dining room is only used for Sunday dinners and holidays.

I have a simple life. I go to school, come home, and start on my homework. If I have time after doing my homework, I play outside. My mom is a great cook, and her meals are delicious. My parents discuss what is happening in our town, country, and world. I often sit there and stare at both of my parents. They know a lot and are willing to share with us. As I got older, I started participating in the dinner discussion by asking questions. I learn a great deal at those dinners; in some ways, I know more than I do in school.

My parents never criticize any of my questions. If I have a problem figuring out how to form a query, one of my parents helps me.

Life Lessons Learned:

My parents' coaching helps me ask more insightful questions throughout my education and life. If people can't figure out how to ask a question, they never get the answer they want.

This question-asking skill is of great use to me in nursing school. I don't pretend I understand because I don't want to be embarrassed. I learn a great deal of information, especially in solving problems, that I use when I become an army nurse.

You may talk with someone about what it was like growing up in their hometown. Many times, the responses could be more pleasant. As I hear these responses, I become reluctant to talk about my wonderful childhood with my sister, brother, parents, and the people of Waterloo, Iowa. I don't want to make people feel wrong about their childhood or parents. For a while, I downplayed the great experiences I had growing up. But then I realized I wasn't true to myself without telling them about my beautiful life experiences. I was diminishing myself in favor of being kind about their problems.

I concluded that I would be honest but short, because short stories with dramatic scenes around the kitchen table might work better. I needed to give my friends a sense of what I had without making them jealous.

I had parents, a mother and a father, but I also had something extraordinary. I had mentors who would talk to me about anything and did their best to answer every question I asked. The example that they set serves me well in life. The best way to get the maximum effective results from people is to educate, train, and encourage them.

CHAPTER 3:

I Love Two Holidays

I love two holidays more than any other: the 4th of July and Christmas. If forced to choose one, I would say Christmas, but that would be tough.

My family is very patriotic, so we love celebrating the 4th of July. My father buys bunting and American flags and decorates the front of our house. He adds bunting to his car, and we drive in the annual parade. After the parade, we have a picnic, and at night we go to the town square for fireworks. After the celebration, we return home to cake and homemade ice cream.

My father does not have to serve in the First World War because he is married with children to support. Even though he doesn't fit in the military, he dramatically respects men and women who risk their lives so that we can be free.

I learn from my Uncle Joe and my mother's brother and cousins, who talk about their time in the trenches in France. My mother took me downtown to shop at the Green & Wilson Department store one day. I see a man on crutches with one of his pants legs rolled up with a large safety pin holding it together. I pull on my mother's arm. She can tell I want to ask her a question, so she bends over and asks if I want to say something. While holding my mom's hand, I point to the gentleman and say, "What happened to his leg?"

My mother doesn't respond right away. Then, she tells me that the gentleman is a hero. His name is Pfc. Edmond Brown, and he served our country in the war. Mr. Brown was severely injured fighting in France. The doctors had to remove a part of his leg to save his life. When somebody serves in the military and is damaged, they eventually return home to their family and their community, who help take care of them. He may get an artificial leg someday and won't need the crutches. Sometimes soldiers get injured and become disabled, which means there are certain things they can't do, so we must help them. All men and women who come back from wars are called veterans. My Uncle Joe is a veteran. I tell Mommy that someday I think I'd like to help veterans and ask if that would be a good thing to do. She says that if I could find a way when I'm all grown up to help veterans, it would be a wonderful thing.

My other favorite holiday is Christmas because, for one reason, I love getting presents. I don't care how big or small they are; give me gifts — the more, the better! We have a family tradition. My dad, brother, and sister go out together to cut down our Christmas tree. Most affordable ornaments are red, green, blue, and yellow, and our tree has lights. We have about 21 lights on the tree in various colors. We don't turn on the lights until Christmas morning. My father has a secret specialty. We put up the tree, lights, and ornaments, and after we go to bed, my father stays up, putting icicles on the tree branches one at a time. When we come down the following day, we have this beautiful, sparkling, shimmering Christmas tree in our front room.

Another thing he does that makes our tree different from everybody else's is to use mica snow. When he finishes the icicles, he stands on a chair, reaches the top of the tree, and pours the mica snow down the tree. It looks like snow on the branches and the ornaments; it even lands on the lights. When he plugs in the lights, the snow changes colors.

The tree goes up a few days before Christmas, but there are no presents under the tree because Santa Claus brings the presents on Christmas Eve. The smell of a Christmas tree in our house and cookies and nut bread baking are magical fragrances to me during Christmas. On Christmas morning, I wake up and go downstairs to see the tree with hundreds of presents under it. Mom makes her fresh biscuits for breakfast, and, as a special treat, we have butter and strawberry jam on Christmas.

Our family goes to church, and I see the nativity scene before the church. It is beautiful, but those presents under the tree are calling all of us, desperately in need to be opened. Christmas Mass is always special, so I wear my best dress and coat. To prolong the anticipation, our parents insist we must change our clothes before we can attack the presents under the tree. Before I go to bed, I lay on the floor under the tree, looking up at all the decorations, snow, and lights. What a fantastic sight! Sometimes I fall asleep, and my dad picks me up and carries me to bed.

When I was nine, Santa Claus brought me a nurse's kit. It is my best present because I can take everybody's temperature and blood pressure and give them pills and pretend shots.

Life Lessons Learned

Family traditions are essential. They re-occur, and even though they may not change, we do. We believe in Santa Claus, and then we don't, but we still love Christmas and other traditions. One of the most critical aspects of traditions is family. When we grow up and move away from our family and hometown, we leave the family behind. As we build our own families in our hometowns or someplace new, we transfer some of our family traditions to the new family and perhaps add some new ones for the next generation.

Traditions are our history, and many of my contemporaries growing up at the same time in different towns all over the country had other Christmas traditions. At Christmas parties or gatherings, we often share stories of what it was like at Christmas in our home growing up. We learn about things other people do that are unique to their culture, and we may decide to add them as new traditions to our family.

One of the hardest things we must do when we get older is being away from our family on Christmas morning. When we have a chance to be with them at Christmas, it is the best Christmas gift.

CHAPTER 4:

St. Mary's Elementary School

I love to learn and do very well in school; at least, my grades say so. On "Parents Night," my folks are told I am first in all my classes. Both of my parents are pleased and proud.

In the fifth grade, I watch some older girls play basketball in the gym. It looks like much hard work and, at the same time, fun. Most other girls in my class are not interested in exercise beyond what the school requires. When I return from Christmas break, I go to Mr. Frank, the coach, and ask if I can learn the game. I am tall for my age and a little skinny. He looks at me, says basketball is challenging, and asks if I am strong. I don't know what he means, so I tell him I don't. He says that they run speed drills at the end of practice, and I should be there at 2:30 in my gym uniform and sneakers to show him what I can do. I am excited. I don't know why I am excited. It is because I will be trying something new that I have never done before. A little before 2:30, I am in the gym sitting on the bleachers, waiting to be told by the coach how I would learn to play basketball.

I didn't say to the coach when we met what my name was. When it is time for me to join in, he yells at me to come over. He asks my name, calls me "Murphy," and points out the brown line painted on the gym floor that goes around the gym. He points out all the girls at the far end of the gym and tells me to stand next to them and do what they do until I can't do it anymore.

So, I run down to the line, the coach blows his whistle, and all the girls take off running.

I stand there frozen for a moment, unsure of what to do next. Then, I take off and join in running as fast as I can along the length of the gym floor. All the girls, me included, touch the brown line, turn around, and run back. I repeat this with them and repeat it again and again. I am exhausted after the third trip. I can't catch my breath. I am hot and sweaty. I don't feel like I can walk, much less run.

The coach comes over to me and tells me that if I want to play basketball, I must keep up with the other girls. I tell the coach that I want to do it, so I will work as hard as possible to see if I can do what he wants. From then on, I run everywhere I need to go. At the next practice, he calls me Murphy again and tells me that running is only one part of the game. Running helps get me more muscular and gets me in the condition to play, but I still need to learn how to shoot, pass, and dribble. The other girls have been playing for a couple of years, but he likes my spirit and agrees that if I put in the time and effort, he'll help make me a basketball player.

The coach is right. I know nothing about basketball, but I am going to learn and learn in a hurry. On my way home, I stopped at the public library to see if they had any books on basketball, and sure enough, they had one called, "Basics of Basketball." After I leave the library and start home, my entire body is aching. I can hardly take a step, but I know I must walk home and will probably have difficulty walking home after basketball practice many more times.

I worked out and practiced with the girls' basketball team, and by the time I was in the eighth grade, I got playing time.

Life Lessons Learned:

The lessons I learned in basketball serve me well later in life when I am an army nurse. When I finish my basketball career, I will be a starter and play the guard position. I am the captain and a team leader on the floor. I am the best shot on the team, and when we need a basket, I am the go-to person. My leadership skills and dead eye serve me well, so not only do I get an excellent education in school, but also I get an excellent education in the gym.

Over my life, I've found myself in positions where I had to lead people. I always look back on my life in that gymnasium, desperately wanting to learn to play basketball. It was a challenge in my life. We may find ourselves with many challenges. How we address conquering those challenges says a great deal about us.

I have been a student all my life. When asked to fulfill a challenge, I need to understand the complexities of the challenge. Once I understand what must be done, I can lay out a plan for training myself to accomplish the challenge.

I didn't start out wanting to be the captain of the team or the go-to shot person. I just wanted to learn how to play basketball. The rest came from my hard work and dedication to achieving the goal. Every challenge we undertake, regardless of whether we are successful or not, we increase a level of knowledge within ourselves that we can draw on for future challenges.

CHAPTER 5:

The Depression

In the spring of 1929, our country's economy is quite the issue. One morning, our parents tell us we will have a family meeting in the dining room that night. They tell us about it just before we leave for school. Having a meeting in the dining room means it is an important meeting. The subject matter is going to be serious. On our way to school, my sister and I discuss what it could be. Patrick isn't old enough to have an opinion; he listens. I'll meet my sister at lunchtime. We continue our morning discussion, trying to figure out the subject of the family meeting that evening.

Walking home from school, we continue discussing what will happen after dinner. I ask my sister if she thinks one of our parents is sick. Finally, the two of us give up, go home, start our homework, and watch the clock on the wall. We smell the meal my mother is cooking and hear our father's car come up the driveway. The dinner is tranquil. We all know something profound will be discussed, and we are scared. None of us want to have a discussion.

Dinner is over, the dishes are cleaned, and our father leads all five of us into the dining room and tells us that they asked for this meeting because they think it is essential we start talking about what's going on in the country.

The headlines in the newspapers talk about the roaring '20s and how good it is everywhere, but my parents think we're in for a severe slowdown in America's economy, which could be very serious. They believe many people might lose their jobs and even their houses. While they can't be sure, if the economy goes wrong, people will want to fix things versus buying new, which bodes well for my father's business and for him to have a reliable income.

Our mom, who works at the dress shop, thinks more women will stop buying fancy dresses, so she goes to the shop owner and says she should start making simple, less expensive dresses. They tell us we might see our neighborhood and school friends' fathers and mothers lose their jobs and that some will have to sell their houses and move away to look for new work.

Father says he thinks we will, for now, be okay, but things could change. He tells us that he and our mother will look for ways to save money, and that would mean they will have to cut back on things. But the three of us need to know that one of the most important things to them is to make sure we all have a good education. He says that no matter how bad it gets, the downturn will not last forever, and we need to be prepared to get a good job when we finish our education.

The college will be expensive, and he asks us to do two things. First, he says to do the very best we can in school. Second, when it comes time to apply to colleges, he wants us to get as much financial aid as possible. Dad asks if we have any questions, and I ask if we will have to move. I am concerned that if we move, I will lose my friends, and especially one friend.

Patrick asks if we will starve. My parents assure him we have plenty to eat, and we will plant a more extensive garden to grow more food. My older sister, who just started her senior year, asks if we should all try to find jobs after school to help pay for things. Dad says that we can get a job if we want, but not at the expense of our grades. They promise we will have regular meetings to update us on what is happening. After Dad says the session is over, we all get up and separate. We all wonder what the future holds.

Life Lessons Learned:

After discussing the possibility of Depression with our family, I decide to start a diary, but I want to do something different. I know many girls keep a daily journal of worthless stuff. I keep an "essential events" diary to write down things that leave an impression on me at the time. I want to have something that I could refer to if I find myself in a situation where I need advice and counsel. The collection of significant events in my diary defined my life.

CHAPTER 6:

Our Lady of Victory High School

When I started my first year of high school, many things changed in the country, as well as for me. One day, I read in the newspaper that on February 14, 1932, in Chicago, seven men were slain in a warehouse at the corner of Dickens and Clark. Five of the seven men killed were part of the North Side Gang. The news report says that there were four killers — two of whom used Thompson submachine guns, while the other two used shotguns. The organized crime gangs were led by George "Bugs" Moran, and the other, on the south side, was led by Al Capone.

The high school basketball coach hears about me from my grade school coach and encourages me to join the team, and I do. My body started to change in the summer between eighth grade and the first year. I had a growth spurt that puts me at 5'8", and I put on about 15 pounds. I am not relatively as lean as I was in elementary school, but I am far from plump. My breasts started to grow, and my mother and I talked about my period and the fact that I would be changing from a child to a woman.

I am a different-looking person at the end of my first year of high school. I am now 5'10". I have put on another 10 pounds, and my breasts are more significant than most girls in the senior class. I also notice something different. During all those years at St. Mary's Elementary School, I didn't pay much attention to boys. When I enter high school, my mother tells me about relationships between boys and girls.

Because of the physical changes that have taken place in my body, along with my red hair and green eyes, many boys, even in the upper classes, come over to talk to me. I get invitations to school dances that my mother and father say no to, but they will consider it after sophomore year.

On March 4, 1929, Herbert Hoover was inaugurated as the 31st president. It is the first presidential election that I follow, but it will not be the last. He was born in West Branch, Iowa, about 100 miles from Waterloo. I find him attractive because he is the first President from Iowa.

Late in my sophomore year, I meet a junior named John Delancey. He is attractive, taller than me, muscular, and a varsity basketball player. When I go to his games to watch him play, I notice that he is perfect. I can tell from seeing him in his uniform that he is well-conditioned. I see all this, but I don't know what to do about it. I know that something makes me feel strange whenever I am around John. We are in the same church, and our families usually attend the same Sunday Mass. I start noticing him everywhere. He has always been there, but now I see him.

One day after school, he approaches me and asks if he can walk me home. I live a few blocks from his house, so we walk the same way. That afternoon, we talk all the way home about all kinds of things. He tells me I am a beautiful young woman with brilliant red hair, deep green eyes, and the rest of me. Then, he quickly changes the subject because he is embarrassed about what he says about me.

The next day, he asks me to go to the Friday night dance, and I don't know what to say. I can't believe I respond, "I'll have to ask my mom and dad." When I say that, I feel like a little kid. I should've said, "Let me think about it, and I'll let you know tomorrow." Then I could go home and ask my parents if it is okay.

My mother says, "I think you should go." My father is more hesitant because he doesn't want to see his little girl grow up. So, I go to the dance with John. We take a break from dancing and go outside, where he kisses me. A boy has never kissed me, so I don't know what to do. Very quickly, I figure out what to do and truly enjoy it. We know we must return to the dance, or somebody will come looking for us to see what we are doing. We dance for a while, have some punch, and talk. It isn't quiet enough to talk on the dance floor, so we go outside another time, kiss again, and go over to sit on a bench.

He looks at me seriously and says, "Have you thought about what you want to do with your life?"

"No, have you?"

"Yes, I want to go away to college to learn to be an engineer."

"What kind of engineer?"

"I want to build bridges, roads, highways, and waterways."

"Wow!"

"Do you realize that you have a little more than two years left in high school, so you need to start thinking about the next step in your life?"

"I may not know what I want to do, but I don't want to stay in Waterloo, get married, have three or four kids, and spend the rest of my life here."

We go back into the dance, and he holds me closer so that our bodies are touching, but I am haunted by his question, "What do you want to do with your life?"

Life Lessons Learned:

Someday, you may find yourself being asked a question by somebody you've never been asked before, and you don't have an answer. These questions help us define who we are and what we want to be in life.

Sometimes, on the surface, the questions are not very complex, but the more we think about them, the more difficult they are for us to answer.

You never know when the questions are coming. You need to understand that no matter how old you are or how much experience you have, someday somebody will ask you that simple but complex question. As we age, the type of question changes because what was potentially devastating as a teenager is no longer relevant. Things can happen in our life, and these simple questions that we must answer can give us insight as to who we are and what we want to do. Be prepared that you may not have the answer right away. It may take some time to figure out what your answer to that question will be.

CHAPTER 7:

A Visit to the Veterans Hospital

Towards the end of the school year, one of my teachers suggested that she would like to schedule a class trip to visit the Veterans Hospital. She wants to try and cheer up the veterans who are staying there. She says it is strictly voluntary. I raise my hand to go to the hospital to see what it is like. I remember the time when I was younger when my mother and I were downtown shopping, and we saw a veteran who had a missing leg. That image has haunted me for a long time.

We are told that before going to the hospital, we will make up gift baskets of fruits and sweets to pass out to the veterans we meet. Willard's grocery store donates the baskets and some contents like fruits and chocolates. The class decorates the baskets with ribbons and bows. I fill mine with sweet things to eat. I take my mom's cookies from the cookie jar. We are going to the hospital Friday morning, so everything must be done by Thursday evening. We aren't finished, and some friends stay until about 7 o'clock, ensuring everything is ready.

I told my mother what I would do, and she is very proud of me and the other students who are going. Mom asks me if the school needs additional chaperones. She is happy to come along. Mom and I go to school the following day, and my mom asks if she can do anything. She is told they can always use an extra chaperone. My mom doesn't sit next to me on the bus. She goes to sit in the back because she doesn't want to embarrass me by sitting next to me.

We arrive at the hospital, and the doctor in charge, Dr. William Smith, meets us and thanks us for coming. All of us are carrying at least two baskets for veterans. Two students are paired up with a parent, nurse, or nurse's aide, and we go to hospital rooms to meet the injured veterans. We have 50 baskets to distribute to the veterans. I have several chances throughout the day to talk to nurses and nurse's aides about what they do.

The more they talk, the more questions I have. They suggest I speak to the head nurse at St. Mary's Hospital. She knows the many different jobs and will give me a good idea of what it's like to work in a hospital. One nurse mentions that St. Mary's has a volunteer aide program I might want to investigate for experience.

A few days later, I call St. Mary's Hospital and ask for the person in charge of nursing. A voice comes on and says she is Sheila Martin. I tell her my name and that I have just been to the VA Hospital and am interested in possibly studying nursing in college.

"I am told I should contact you to talk about nursing and the possibility of becoming a volunteer to get a feel for what nurses do in a general hospital and see if I am interested in becoming a nurse. Miss Martin, when should I come to see you?"

"How about next Tuesday after school? Can you be here by four o'clock?"

"That shouldn't be a problem. I will see you next Tuesday at 4 p.m."

"I look forward to seeing you and trying to help make your decision."

I told my mom what I was doing, and she thought volunteering at the hospital was a good idea to see if I would like it.

Life Lessons Learned:

I learn from this experience that having people who can give me objective information will help me make better decisions. I know I will make mistakes, but gathering information minimizes errors.

Asking questions helps us gather information. The more information we collect, the better the decision will be. The person you are asking the question of may have some insight into an answer to your question. Just because that person answered the question doesn't mean you can't ask them more questions.

I didn't know when somebody asked me what I wanted to be as a young girl in high school for the longest time. I didn't know. So, when somebody asked the question, the answer I had wasn't what they were looking for. When I finally decided what I wanted to be when I grew up, I could say, "I want to be a nurse." I wasn't sure if I wanted to be a nurse, but it gave me some focus and an option to explore.

CHAPTER 8:

Good Catholic Girls

I meet John after dinner and tell him everything that happened that day. "You asked me at the dance last week what I would do with my life."

I am so excited that I throw my arms around his neck. He puts his arms around my waist and pulls me tightly into him. We stop talking, and our lips meet. This kiss is better than the ones at the dance. He holds me so tight that my breasts are pressed against his chest. The combination of our lips and bodies being so close sparks a flame in us. I feel like a fire inside of me is growing in intensity the longer we hold each other.

I realize that no matter how much I like the feelings, the message that I've heard dozens upon dozens of times is that good Catholic girls don't have sex until after they're married. Ingrained in my brain, this message causes me to pull away from John. He is startled by how quickly we separate and says, "What's wrong?"

"This is wrong, at least for me. The passion of our bodies close together is not something we should be experiencing. I must go." I quickly run inside the house.

Later that evening, I thought about apologizing to John, but we have a party line, and you can never tell who might be listening. I decide to call him and have a very brief conversation. I say, "John, I know things did not go well today, but could we talk tomorrow after school?"

I wait for John to respond. It seems like forever until he finally says, "Yes, I'll see you tomorrow after school."

"Good night."

I didn't sleep well that night trying to figure out what I would say to John about our somewhat intimate encounter. I know that teenagers who are rapidly developing physically find that their bodies sometimes work ahead of their brains.

My participation in school the next day isn't scholarship quality. Based on stories I hear, I know the danger of other girls who go too far. They find themselves pregnant and must drop out of school. I already told John that I didn't want to graduate from high school, get married, and have kids. If we went "all the way," that was a possibility. So, I decided I would look for an opportunity in the conversation with John to tell him that we will have to set limits on ourselves physically if we continue our relationship; I am not going to get pregnant and drop out of school. If he doesn't accept those terms, as much as I will miss him, that is how it must be.

Our houses are not that far from the school. It is a pleasant day, so I suggest to John that we go to the bench in the park at the end of Myrtle Avenue. He agrees, and we walk together, but I don't say anything until we get to the bench. I tell him that I think he is handsome and beautiful sexually, but I can't have sex with him no matter how much I like him. I will not risk getting pregnant and destroying my dreams.

He sits there for a moment before he responds. "You are a beautiful young woman with an exceptional body, and anybody would want to make love with you. I'm not sure that most of those people would be concerned about your feelings, though. They would want to have sex with any beautiful young woman. I suggest we continue our relationship and see where it goes. If, at some point in the future, you feel that you would like to have sex with me, I can assure you I will have sex with you. Besides, I have a latex condom that goes over me and stops the sperm from entering you during sex."

I am embarrassed at what John is saying because I have never heard of condoms. If it is true, it seems that if we decide to have sex and use a condom, I would be safe. "Let's see how things go. No promises. Agreed?"

"Yes."

I would need a trip to the library to research condoms and their safety.

Life Lessons Learned:

I learned that emotions can be a powerful driver of what we do. Emotions that are driven by hormones are even more powerful. Sometimes our body tells us that it is okay to do things when our brain tells us a different message. As a high school teenager, I was concerned about having sex, getting pregnant, and having to leave school. Would the lives of girls who did that have been different if they hadn't gotten pregnant? It's hard to say, but they will always wonder, "What if...?"

Giving in to the pressure to do things, sex included, because we want to please somebody else may ultimately make us feel disappointed in ourselves. As we get older and go out in the real world to make our way, we may find ourselves in situations where we must consider doing something that may not be right. We may have regrets after we do it. We may gain influence, power, or money in deciding, but the outcome may not make us happy. One of the most significant questions in life is, can I be satisfied with what I am doing? And if I'm not, can I have the courage to change and do something different?

CHAPTER 9:

St. Mary's Hospital

I had difficulty sleeping the night before my St. Mary's Hospital visit. The plan is for me to go to the hospital after school and meet the woman in charge of nursing around 4 o'clock. I go to the front desk, where a sign says "information."

I indicate to the woman on the other side of the desk that I am here to see Sheila Martin. The young woman calls and tells me that Miss Martin will be down shortly and for me to sit in the chairs against the window.

This is only the second time I've ever been in a hospital besides the VA Hospital. I sit in an uncomfortable chair that has a table beside it. On the table are some outdated magazines. About five minutes later, Miss Martin enters the lobby, and the woman behind the desk points to me. Miss Martin is wearing a cap, shoes, and stockings in a white nurse's uniform. It seems she is white all over.

Miss Martin is about five foot, six inches tall, in her 40's, and has a nice figure. She extends her hand; I take it, and we shake. She sits in the chair on the other side of the table.

"So, you're considering the possibility of attending nursing school. Is that correct?"

"I'm thinking about it. I want to learn more about nursing. Last week, I was at the VA Hospital and watched nurses interact with patients. I had a warm feeling about what was taking place. I decided I needed to ask how I could learn more, which brought me here to St. Mary's Hospital."

"You understand that we're not a teaching hospital, that we're just a regular hospital? You would have to attend a nursing school to be trained as a nurse."

"Yes, I understand. I'd like to learn more about what nurses do to decide whether I want to be a nurse."

"Well, what do you know about nursing?"

"All I know is what I saw last week at the VA. That was the first time I've ever been in a hospital."

"Is it alright if I call you Miss Murphy?"

"That seems so formal, but I guess it's okay."

"Miss Murphy, I've given some thought about what the best way would be to show you what nurses do. I've arranged to take you on a hospital tour to show you the different operating departments. You'll get information on what happens in each department by taking a tour of some departments."

"Are there many departments at St. Mary's?"

"Yes, there are quite a few."

"Let's start where many people come into the hospital – the emergency room. Shall we go?"

"Yes, please."

We go down a very long hallway to a set of double doors. Above the doors is a sign that says, "Emergency Room."

"Before we go in, I must tell you that you must stay close to me so that we won't interfere with patient care. You can ask me questions, and I will do my best to answer them, but we are here to watch how an emergency room operates."

Miss Martin opens the doors in front of us and leads me to an area next to the sign-in desk. All the medical people in the emergency room wear light blue tops and bottoms. I later find out their clothes are called scrubs. People enter the emergency room walking, in a wheelchair, or on a stretcher. Sometimes, many people come at once, Miss Martin tells me.

I see a man who is talking to a person. I think a nurse is asking him about his medical history. Then suddenly, a stretcher pushed by emergency squad people comes crashing through the door with a man on it who has blood all over him. He is on oxygen, and the nurse tells them to take the patient to ER 1. I am in the emergency room for about 20 minutes, and in that time, I see 25 people come in. It looks hectic. The nurses and doctors do their best to treat the patients as quickly as possible.

Miss Martin says, "We need to move on, so follow me." We go down another hallway to an elevator, which we take up to the nursery. There is a glass wall between the babies and us to protect the babies from germs carried by visitors. In some cases, the nurses are feeding the babies a bottle.

Miss Martin says, "Those babies who are not getting a bottle will be taken to their mother's rooms so they can feed from the breast." There must be 15 babies in the nursery. Miss Martin continues, "That's about an average number of babies in the nursery daily. It would be best to remember that the nursery must have nurses present 24 hours a day, seven days a week. The same applies to the emergency room and anywhere else in the hospital where patients need care. It's time for us to move on to our next department."

We walk down a hallway, peek into a room, and see a young woman nursing her baby. It is a beautiful sight. I try to imagine myself someday holding a baby to my breast. We go back to the elevator and then up to the surgical floor. "This is where we have operating rooms, recovery rooms for patients, and patient rooms. We can't go into the rooms, but we can walk by, and you'll see nurses at work."

After about 10 minutes, we have one more stop. We get in the elevator and go up one more floor. She says, "This is the intensive care floor," when we exit the elevator. "This is for people who are sick. Some will die here. We take care of them just like any other patient in the hospital." We will walk down the center of the hallway, and if a door opens, we can see patients. "I want you to see another part of this floor before we leave."

I can't imagine what she wants to show me. We walk down to the end of the hallway and to a large room with 12 plastic boxes. I investigate some of them, and they have babies in them. I ask her, "What is this?"

"This is the intensive care for newborn babies who are sick. They need much care, and sometimes one baby will have multiple nurses taking care of it."

I stand in the doorway, looking at the tiny babies struggling for life.

"It's time to go," she says.

We go to the elevator and take it down three floors to her office.

"So, Miss Murphy, that was a quick tour," Miss Martin says. I look at my watch. The tour took 2½ hours. "Do you have any questions?"

"Yes, I have several. Do you have any information on your volunteer program?"

She opens her desk drawer, pulls out a brochure, and hands it to me.

"How much time do I have to commit to your volunteer program?"

Miss Martin replies, "Ten hours a week is a good schedule for a volunteer. You can work more than that, but less than ten hours a week doesn't help the nurses much."

"What do you think my job opportunities would be if I graduate from a nursing school?"

"Miss Murphy, you can get a job anywhere in the country. There's a very critical shortage of nurses."

"I would like to return and spend a few more minutes in the emergency room. If I work as a volunteer, can I spend part of my time in the emergency room?"

"Yes, I'll be more than happy to take you back for another visit. As to your question of being a volunteer in the emergency room, that might be possible after you have some experience."

I go back to the emergency room for another half an hour. I thank Miss Martin for her time and say, "May I ask you one more question?"

"Certainly."

"If I want to go to a top-notch nursing school, assuming I have the grades, where would you recommend I go?"

"That is easy. St. James Hospital School of Nursing in Chicago. If you come back, we have some nurses here on our staff from St. James, and I could arrange for you to talk with them."

As I walk to the bus station and ride the bus home, I decide that day that I want to be a nurse. More importantly, I want to be an ER nurse and attend the St. James School of Nursing in Chicago.

Life Lessons Learned:

In a few short years, my training at St. James for the ER would serve me and my patients well.

Did you ever have a good day, the kind of day when everything went right, and you were happy? Those are the days that we live for. They may be complex and challenging. But when we succeed in the challenge, we feel good about ourselves. We may be lucky that others recognize our accomplishments and congratulate us on our success. Often, that doesn't happen because we are the only one who knows how happy we are with what we've done.

I often wonder how some days are so great and others are terrible. Is it just luck, or did I do something to screw up? I never really figured that out, and I wish you luck if you do because many people would love to have that secret.

Usually, we have a good day because we accomplish something; it doesn't have to be spectacular, just something small. I believe that when we have a terrible day, that experience leaves an impression on our soul, and when we have a good day, it heals our soul.

CHAPTER 10:

Talk with John

When I get home from the hospital, my family has finished eating dinner. My mother has saved a plate of food for me in the oven. My mother sets the container on the table and sits across from me. In a few moments, my father comes into the kitchen, sits at the table, and asks, "How was your visit?"

The question is the key that opens the floodgates. I tell my parents as much as I can remember. I experienced this today. I don't take a breath for a long time.

When I finish, my father asks, "Are you returning?"

I don't hesitate. "Yes, I am, and I'm considering volunteering."

My father says, "Good for you. If this is what you want to do, we're behind you 100%."

"Thank you so much. I have a brochure that I need to look at, and then I'll pass it on to you and Mom."

"Your mother and I look forward to seeing it. Do you have homework to do?"

"Yes, but I have one other thing I have to do first; it won't take long."

Our phone is on a table in the hallway. When anyone is on the phone, their voice echoes throughout the house. I pick up the phone and dial John's number. He answers the phone, and in an excited voice, I ask, "Can you come over for a little bit?"

"Yes. I want to hear about your day. I'll be there in 20 minutes."

I finish my food and put my dishes in the sink. I go to my room to ensure I look nice for John. I go downstairs and sit on the front porch, waiting for my knight in shining armor.

He comes down the sidewalk and walks up the steps. He comes over to the swing, bends over, and kisses me. That distracts me in a good way. I kiss him back as he kisses me. I can see him look in the window next to the swing to see if my parents are sitting in the living room. They aren't. He bends over once more to kiss me but gently puts his hand on my breast. That startles me.

"What are you doing? Stop that." He takes his hand away, gives me a gentle kiss, and sits on the swing beside me.

He says to me, "Tell me about your visit."

I want to tell him so many things, but first, I must ask him, "Do you remember the night of the dance when I told you that I didn't know what I wanted to do with my life? I needed help answering your question."

"Yes. Sure, I do."

"Well, John, I think I found my answer today. I want to be a nurse, and I want to work in an ER department. I think I even know where I want to go to school."

I can't stop talking. After about 20 minutes, John leans over and kisses me again. He says, "I'm so proud of you."

I quickly kiss him back, but something stirs inside me again, only more robust, and I kiss him again. He takes his hand and puts it on my breast, but then he jumps back because he is so surprised. When he reached for my breast again, I forcibly turn away, and he says, "Why did you do that?"

"I understand I'm attractive to you. You excite me sexually too. But my body is not a toy you can play with anytime. I understand that physical attraction is natural for us. Your body is not my toy, either. We have broken that invisible barrier and can't return to how we were before. I would be lying if I told you I didn't enjoy being touched by you and touching you. We must be careful and, most importantly, respectful of each other. We have started down a path that may be difficult for both of us. I like you, but I'm not ready to give myself to you."

After that difficult discussion, I told John I was exhausted and needed to sleep. I give him a quick kiss and watch him walk down the street. As I walk up the steps to the front door, I ask myself, *Have we moved to the next level in our relationship? Will we ever have a genuine relationship?* Only time will tell.

Life Lessons Learned:

That night, I learned that our passions are a powerful thing. Having control over them is essential, but sometimes you just must let go. In so doing, there may be a price to pay. Passions are more than sexual desire. Those other passions will come to the surface. I will have to learn to control them.

CHAPTER 11:

A Serious Conversation with Kelly

I walk up the stairs to the bedroom I share with my sister Kelly with a lot on my mind. When I arrive, she sits on her bed reading a book. Kelly is three years older than me. She has already graduated from high school and is going to secretarial school. Kelly works part-time as a secretary to a junior executive at a local insurance company. She has a steady boyfriend, Ted Smith. I like Ted. He is always taking Kelly out to dinner or a movie. They fit together very well.

She looks up at me when I come into the room. She has a smile on her face when she says, "Did he touch you?"

I don't know for sure what she is talking about.

"I know he put his hand on one of your breasts."

"How do you know that?"

"Take a look in the mirror. You can tell because your blouse is all messed up on the left side."

I am embarrassed, but I use that as an opening to ask her, "Have you ever had a messed-up blouse?"

She smiles and somewhat laughs. "All the time. It's just part of growing up, and if you have a nice body like both of us, many young men want to get their hands on you."

I am somewhat shocked at what she is saying. "You seem cavalier about the whole thing."

"Little sister, I'm not trying to be cavalier. I'm just dealing with the reality of relationships today. You have a sheltered life in school. You're not dealing with the validity of the world out there. From the beginning of time, men have always been after women. Sexual tension makes hormones rage, especially in young people. Sexual tension is not the only pressure that young people are dealing with.

People are talking about the possibility of a severe economic downturn that could lead to an economic depression. You know that Mom and Dad have talked with us about this, and I think it will happen. You need to stop off at the newspaper section on your next visit to the library and start reading the big city newspapers. You'll see stories about the civil unrest in Europe. We just finished one world war, which was supposed to be the war to end all wars, and now we're talking about a new war. Our nation lost many men in the war. Many husbands, brothers, and boyfriends died for this country. When men went to war, they didn't know if they were coming back. They had girlfriends who didn't know if they would ever see their men again. Passion ran high, and many people had sex they probably shouldn't have had. Ted and I have not had sex, but if our country goes to war and Ted is drafted before we get married, I will have sex with him. I don't mean to be casual about what is happening between you and John. Both of you are at an age where your hormones are exploding. He looks at you and sees the beautiful young woman you have become. You are still developing, and he wants you now.

I think relationships between men and women have created many problems in history. John wants you, and his signal to you was his act of touching you. Then, you threw him a monkey wrench by turning him down, and he doesn't know what to do. Little sister, that was brilliant. I wish I had thought of that with Ted or the other boys. So, right now, you are wondering what you should do. Should you break it off with John, or will you progress to become more intimate with each other? And that doesn't necessarily have to be sex.

The time will come when you must decide. Do you want to give yourselves to each other? If you do have sex, what happens next? If you make that decision, I have one crucial message unless you want to get pregnant — use a condom. You have laid down, for now, the ground rules. You and your body are not his toy, and he and his body are not. That is such a great line. I wish I would have thought of it. You are brilliant. Enjoy this time in your life with John, but know that he will not be the only love of your life."

Life Lessons Learned:

We all need a road map to help us get where we are going, and the suggestions from my big sister will come in handy. In life, we meet people and immediately find a bond; sometimes, it will be sexual, and other times not. I believe in having a rich and whole life. We need both.

CHAPTER 12:

A Conversation with my Biology Teacher

The next day, I went in to see my biology teacher. I want to schedule an appointment with her about college, nursing school, and John. Miss Withers is my teacher but doesn't look much older than my sister Kelly. I like her a lot. She makes things interesting. She gives us many research assignments that need to be done at the library. I know my way around the library. I could find the subject matter of any project she would give me faster than anybody in the class.

I will finish first in the class by the end of the school year. I knock on her door, and her voice says, "Come in." I go in.

"Good morning, Miss Withers. I have a few things to discuss with you. Would you have time this afternoon to talk?"

"Sure, come by at 3:15. I look forward to helping you if possible."

At lunchtime, I thought about what I wanted to talk about with Miss Withers, and I decided that talking about John would be last and only if there was time.

The school day ends at 3 p.m. I hear the bell ring and look at the clock on the wall. It is 3 o'clock, so I have 15 minutes to meet Miss Withers. I take my books and drop them off in my locker, and I stop by the water fountain. It is about 3:10. I walk down the hallway to Miss Withers classroom.

I knock on the door and hear, "Come on in, Mary Ellen."

She is not at her desk but sitting at a student's desk, asking me to sit across from her. I feel very much at ease because of our seating arrangement. Having our desks next to each other makes me think of my conversation with Kelly the night before when we talked sister to sister.

"What's on your mind? How can I help you?"

"Miss Withers, I have been thinking about college, and more specifically, I've been thinking about nursing school. If I can complete the science subjects successfully, I want to become an ER nurse."

"That's an ambitious goal. An ER nurse must focus her attention for extended periods and deal with success and some disappointments. Why do you think you want to be an ER nurse? Hospitals have many different departments. They each require nurses. The skill level for newborn nurses differs from those in an emergency room."

"What I like about the emergency room is that you have to make decisions quickly because those decisions often turn out to be a matter of life or death."

"Based on your scores in my biology class, you are an exceptional student. I do not doubt that you could easily handle the academic nursing subject. I wonder if you will be able to handle the trauma, anxiety, and depression, especially seeing the death of a patient that you work on in the ER."

"That's a tough question. It's something that I think about. I will sign up for the summer volunteer program at St. Mary's Hospital here in Waterloo. I've been assured that I will get time working in the ER."

"That seems like a great plan so that if you don't like it, you still have the rest of your junior and senior year to try something different."

"I agree, I think it is a good plan, and I appreciate your support. If I decide to go to nursing school, assuming I keep my grades up, would you be willing to write a letter of reference?"

It didn't take her long to reply. "Of course I will. Anything I can do that helps you further your education, I want to do."

I've got to find out if she has the time to talk about John, so I ask, "I know you've already given me half an hour. Do you have time for one more question?"

"Not a problem. I don't have to leave here until 5 o'clock."

I say to myself, *I hope that's enough time.* "Most girls my age are changing from a little girl to a young woman. A young man complicates that transition, which is still going on for me." I see a smile spread across her face that says she's been here before, having a conversation with girls like me and in her own life. I can tell by looking at her face that she still has vivid memories of her own experience.

"How can I help you?"

"I have a boyfriend who is a junior. Our relationship just turned to petting. I've told him I don't want to get pregnant, but my emotions and hormones are driving me to have sex with him. We recently had an incident that I was uncomfortable with, and I told him that, but later, he touched me again, and I felt differently. We have discussed more than once that I don't want to get pregnant and leave school because it would destroy my dream of being a nurse. I love Waterloo. It is a great place to grow up, but I want to see at least some of the world before settling down and having children. Getting pregnant in high school short circuits a degree in nursing and working in an ER."

"Has your boyfriend talked to you about using condoms to protect you from becoming pregnant?"

She was surprised when I answered, "Yes. My sister told me that if I'm going to have sex to use a condom."

"That's good. Have you talked about the reliability of condoms? They tend to crack and break, so they can leak. Is this young man your first encounter?"

"Yes. He's a junior."

"Does he want to stay in Waterloo, or does he have similar plans to yours?"

"Funny you should ask, because we talked recently that he has a plan, and at that time, I had none. Now, I think we both have a plan."

"Since he will be leaving school before you, what do you think will happen to the relationship when he's away at college, and you're still in your last year of high school? If you can keep a long-distance relationship and go off to college in a different city than where he is, will your relationship survive? You need to sit down and discuss where this relationship is going. You are close intimate friends, but each of you will go your own way in the next few years. Do you think you may still feel great affection for each other after three or four years of college? I think you're way too young to make that decision. I think you are in a physical and emotional growth spurt. You need to understand what's driving your feelings and learn as much as you can about him, but don't make commitments that you could regret for the rest of your life. Neither one of you know who you might meet at college who could be the right person for you. You both have much life to live. I want you to enjoy as much of it as possible with the least heartache. Does that help?"

"Yes. Thank you for bringing so many things into focus. I will have a conversation, perhaps more than one, with my boyfriend both about today and the future."

I thank her again and notice it is almost 4:30. I go to my locker, get my books and coat, and slowly close the locker door. I walk down the long hallway while thinking about the excellent information and recommendations she gave me.

Life Lessons Learned:

I learned that day that I am in more control than I thought. If a plan is going to be successful, all the parties must buy into the project. We can only believe it sometimes today. We must also train ourselves to try and look to the future.

CHAPTER 13:

First Day at St. Mary's Hospital

The last few weeks have been hectic. I speak with St. Mary's, talk with Miss Martin, and say, "I want to come be a volunteer and see how it feels for me."

I send a letter to St. James Hospital Nursing School in Chicago requesting enrollment information and about their program. I also call St. Ambrose School of Nursing to get their data to compare the two programs. Is there a significant difference in St. Mary's in Chicago? Final exams for the school year will be coming up in about two weeks, along with the Junior-Senior prom. John asks me to be his date for the dance, and Mom offers to make me a dress. I only see John once over the two-week period. I miss him.

I'm looking forward to the prom and a long summertime with John.

In my call with Miss Martin at St. Mary's Hospital, I tell her I want to come in and work as a volunteer. She is thrilled. I tell her I can work three hours a day, three days a week, and three hours on Saturday.

She says, "Next Monday is your first day."

"I'm excited about being at the hospital and helping in any way I can."

I know it'll be a while before I can be in the ER. I want to learn from Miss Martin what I must do to spend time in the ER. After the first week, she promised that if I still am interested in being a volunteer, we would talk about a plan. She says that she will help me get into the ER at least one session a week.

The day before my first volunteer day is Sunday. My whole family attends church, and John, his mother, and his father are at the same mass. After mass, we tell our parents we will walk home from church. After we are out of sight of our parents and the church, we kiss, but no touching, and I am happy.

I tell John, "I know you want to touch me, and I want to touch you. Thank you for respecting my wishes. I have no doubt we will be together sometime soon. I know I told you I will volunteer at St. Mary's Hospital. Tomorrow is my first day."

"Can I call you after you get home so you can tell me what your day was like?"

"It's better for me to call you because I don't know for sure when I'll get home. It should be after 7 o'clock. Is that okay?"

"That's fine, just call me when you get home."

That night was difficult to sleep. John was on my mind, but taking center stage was what would happen tomorrow at St. Mary's. In my conversation with Miss Martin, she didn't tell me what I would do. My mind was wondering about all the possibilities. I'm a person who wants to know as much as possible about what could happen.

I went to the library and found a book about the departments in a hospital. I studied the book, so I know something about all the departments. I don't have an actual activity to prepare for. I prepared for many different scenarios by reading the book. It is late into the night before I finally go to sleep. When I wake up at my usual time, I am tired. I know it will be a long day with school and volunteering at the hospital, but I don't care. I am excited.

After school, I take the crosstown bus that stops right in front of the hospital. I walk up the front steps into the lobby, go to the reception desk, and ask for Miss Martin.

"Please tell her that Mary Ellen Murphy is here."

Before three, Miss Martin exits the elevator, walks over to me, and says, "Welcome. I'm glad to see you. First, we must go to personnel. You must fill out a few forms, and I will pick you up at 3:30."

At 3:30, Miss Martin comes into personnel and asks, "Are you finished?"

"Yes, I am."

"Okay, let's go."

"Where are we headed?"

"Do you remember when I said the ER was where many patients enter the hospital?"

"Yes, I do."

"Well, that wasn't correct. Eventually, everybody who checks into the hospital must go through the admissions department, including those who come into the ER. Admissions are where we gather a lot of patient information that will go into their files, but it's not real medical history. That comes later. I have a map that I'm going to give you of all the departments in the hospital, because part of your job in admissions will be to take the patients to the correct departments in the hospital. You will learn quickly where all the departments are. This map will be a great help to you for a little while. The admissions department is where you will be working for several weeks. Sometimes, it will be hectic, and sometimes it will be very slow. When you're done today, I will meet with you to see how your shift went, and I'll try and help you with any answers to your questions."

Life Lessons Learned:

The unknown can be scary at times, but it can also be exciting, especially if you're doing something you might like to do for the rest of your life. I know there are departments in the hospital that I have no interest in, but I told Miss Martin I'll do my best on any assignment.

Sometimes you learn more from doing something you don't like. I know there will be people on my staff who don't want to be where they are. However, my job is to get the most I can from every one of those people.

CHAPTER 14:

My First Shift

When I left the hospital, Miss Martin gave me two red and white striped jumpers to wear to the hospital. She also provides me two unique, white, short-sleeve blouses with a red and white volunteer patch on the right shoulder. I add white anklets and some black flats. My mom suggests I wear a sweater just in case it's cold.

I think about what I will be doing during class, and I'm not paying great attention, but there's little class time left. Saturday night is the prom. Graduation is the following Saturday, and then final exams, and we're done.

The school day is over, and a new adventure begins. Fortunately, I can pick up the bus right in front of the school, and the same bus ultimately takes me to St. Mary's Hospital. The bus takes forever to get to the hospital, but really it's only about 25 minutes. I get off the bus and walk up to the front door. I go to the reception desk a little before three. I tell the receptionist that I'm here to see Miss Martin. I go over to a chair and sit and wait for Miss Martin to come down. I don't have to wait long.

She greets me and says, "Welcome to the hospital. Are you ready to go to work?"

"Yes. Where will I be working today?"

"I'm going to take you to a place that generally is not considered exciting, but it's essential. You're going to work this week in the admissions department. You're going to learn how to fill out the admission forms. How to ask about some level of personal history. You will take the patients in a wheelchair to where they need to go. Not a glamor job. It is important for the patient because it is the first step the patient will take in the hospital, and how you treat the patient establishes the hospital's reputation. Miss Murphy, somebody once said that you never get a second chance to make a first impression. Your job in admissions is to help make the right first impression with the people we serve."

I follow Miss Martin, but I'm thinking about what she said. I represent one of the early impressions of the hospital. I better do an excellent job because they won't let me return if I mess up. We walk down the long hallway. I'm learning that hospitals have a lot of long hallways. We approach a door, Miss Martin pushes the door open, and we're in the hospital's main lobby. We come up to a door I've seen every time I've come to the hospital but have yet to learn where it went. She opens the door, and we walk together to this vast room with a dozen stations where people from the hospital talk with patients.

She takes me over to a desk, and I see a small sign on the front that says, "Miss Gregory, Admissions."

"Miss Gregory, I'd like you to meet Miss Mary Ellen Murphy, a new volunteer. She is thinking about going to nursing school. She thinks spending some time here will help her decide based on her experience in our hospital."

"I think that's a smart idea."

"I will leave you two together, and you come to see me, Miss Murphy, when you finish your shift. I want to hear all about your first day."

"Do you prefer to be called Miss Murphy, Mary, or Mary Ellen?"

"Mary Ellen is fine with me, Miss Gregory."

"Why don't you call me Margaret?"

"Perhaps soon I will call you Margaret, but until I prove myself to you, I would much prefer to call you Miss Gregory."

"That's fine. So, I understand you're thinking about becoming a nurse. You're doing a smart thing by visiting a hospital to see if you like the environment before applying to a nursing school. Is there a particular kind of nursing you'd like to do?"

I respond quickly, "Yes, Miss Gregory. I want to be an Emergency Room nurse."

"Why did you pick the emergency room?"

"It seems that much action takes place in the ER."

"I agree, but it's a challenging department, full of good and bad emotions. Admissions are nowhere near as exciting as the ER, but we do important work. So, let's get started."

We both get up, and Miss Gregory leads me to the entrance. She points to a box with a strip of paper coming out of the bottom with a number on it. She tears one off.

"Every person who comes into the admissions department must get a number. Looking around the walls, you will see a sign with the number on it. When an administrator like me is free, we look at the movement and call out the number. We stand up so people can see us in the waiting area, and then they come over and sit in the chair in front of us. Every patient must fill out this form, and it's straightforward. It asks for your name and address. There will be some information about why the patient is coming to the hospital. Somebody may be coming in to have surgery. We make that notation on the form, and then we ask for their doctor's name. Once the form is signed, we put it on a clipboard. We help the patient get into a wheelchair and take them to the correct floor. In this case, the surgical floor.

I tell the receiving nurse that we have Ms. or Mr. so-and-so here for surgery. The nurse will tell us where to take the patient. If necessary, we will help the patient into a chair and let the nurse know that we delivered the patient and anything they brought along. We will say goodbye to the patient and return with the wheelchair. Any questions?"

"It seems pretty straightforward. Where can I go wrong?"

"That's a smart question. Many volunteers have never worked with wheelchairs. One of the most common problems is that volunteers forget to use the brakes. Remember, there's a brake for each wheel, so make sure you take off both brakes."

"Good to know, thank you. Anything else?"

"Yes. Things can quickly get out of hand in maneuvering the wheelchair. One of the common mistakes is to cut a corner too sharply. You can tip over the wheelchair and possibly injure the patient. For now, do it slow and deliberate."

"I can do that. I can be slow and deliberate."

"Well, let's get our first patient and see how things go."

Mrs. Pam Smith is sitting in the chair across from Miss Gregory, and I have my form, which I'm filling out when Miss Gregory does the official document. She is filling in the answers to the questions she's asking Miss Smith. I give my paper and clipboard to Miss Gregory; she gives me hers. I assist Mrs. Smith into the wheelchair. We are going to the surgery floor.

I take out the little map Miss Martin gave me, showing me directions to the surgery floor. I'm cautious and very slow in delivering Mrs. Smith safely to the surgery floor. I am gone for about 30 minutes, and when I return, Miss Gregory and I review the forms I filled out to ensure I did it correctly. She told me I did an excellent job. So, for the rest of my shift, we check in people, fill out the forms, have the patients sign them, and of course, I deliver the patient to the proper area in the hospital.

In my three-hour shift, I handle six incoming patients. When my time is up, I tell Miss Gregory that I have to leave and that I might see her tomorrow, depending upon where Miss Martin wants to send me. I return to Miss Martin's office, and we chat about my day. I tell her I'm beginning to figure out the layout of the hospital without the map.

I say goodbye to Miss Martin. I tell her that I will see her tomorrow at 3 o'clock. I go to the bus stop and wait for the bus to take me home. I must wait a few minutes until one arrives. On the bus ride, I play back in my mind all I accomplished today.

Life Lessons Learned:

I learned on my first day that order and discipline make things work reliably, and without both, you have chaos. If you have confusion in a hospital, people can potentially die. Doctors take an oath not to harm, and so do I.

CHAPTER 15:

Conversation with Everybody in the Family

When I get home, my family is at the front door waiting for me. Everybody wants to know how my first day was at St. Mary's. Patrick wants to know if I killed anybody. Kelly wants to see if I met any cute boys. I suggest that we all go to the kitchen so I can have something to eat, and I will tell them about my day.

I tell them, "I worked in the admissions department. I got to move patients to their rooms in wheelchairs. I met many nurses, doctors, and patients. I learned you must get the information right because people's lives may be at stake."

I finish my dinner, thank my mom for saving it for me, and the discussion ends. I thank everybody for their interest and say, "We can do it again tomorrow night if you want, but if you don't mind, I need to make a phone call. I have homework, and then I must get to bed."

I go into the hallway and dial John's number. He answers on the first ring. We spend about 10 minutes talking about our day. It is lovely to hear his voice. I love how supportive he is of what I am doing.

"As much as I want to stay on the phone with you, I still have homework. I'll see you in the morning on the way to school. Good night."

I go back into the kitchen, and my mother is still there, so I ask her to sit down at the table with me. "Is there something else you need to tell me?"

"No, but I do have a question for you. How's my prom dress coming?"

"I want to do one more fitting with you tomorrow, and then I'll finish it on Wednesday. I think it's one of the finest dresses I've ever made, and if I may say, I think many girls will be very jealous. It's going to be elegant and sophisticated for you."

I thank my mother. "I'm sure it will be beautiful. I can't wait to see what it looks like on me. Now, I have to get to my homework."

I go to my bedroom, finish my homework, and prepare for bed. Then, I crawl into bed and turn out the light on the bedside table, thinking I will quickly fall asleep because I am so tired. However, I just lay in bed thinking about everything that happened today. In some respects, while it was a great day, I am out of control. I need to think more about my schedule, so I use less energy. I promise to work on that on the bus to the hospital. I realize that school will be out for the summer in about two weeks. As I close my eyes, my thoughts turn to John and him holding and kissing me.

The prom will be a memorable night for both of us.

Life Lessons Learned:

Somebody once said that if you find yourself in a hole, stop digging. As my life became more complex, I realized I could only do so much. I must use my time wisely. I must remember when I should stop digging.

CHAPTER 16:

The Prom

On Wednesday night, I try on the prom dress in my mother's bedroom. She has a full-length mirror on the wall so I can see what the dress looks like on me. The upper portion from the waist up fits comfortably around my torso. There are inch-wide shoulder straps and a modest scoop down the back and the front. The dress is tucked in at the waist and falls straight to the floor. It looks like an Asian influence in the design of the dress. The dress is made of white satin, and it is beautiful.

John borrows his father's car the night of the prom and picks me up at seven. The prom starts at 7:30, so we have plenty of time to get to the gym. The theme is "Under the Sea." Fishing nets, lifesavers, and lobster traps are all over the room. The tables have light blue tablecloths and tall white candles in an arrangement of white carnations. There are colored lights of light blue, red, and white in the corner of the gym. The blue and red lights are soft, not harsh. We arrive, find our table, and immediately go to the dance floor. There's a live band playing music. John and I start to dance. He puts his arms around my waist, pulls me close, and then we kiss.

The flame that has been there before is burning bright tonight. As we move around the dance floor, I see girls and boys looking at us. I can tell they are looking at my dress. Wearing the dress makes me feel and look like I am older and more sophisticated than I am. I always loved to dress up as a little girl. I am doing it for real tonight in a custom-made dress.

We dance a couple more dances before I whisper into John's ear, "I'm hungry."

"Me too; let's go to the food table. I can see they are serving dinner."

We eat back at our table. Before returning to the dance floor, we step outside for some fresh air. John takes my hand in his, and we walk over to a park bench and sit for a moment.

"I have something for you."

"What?"

John reaches into the pocket of his tux, takes out a small box, and opens it. I turn the box around so I can see what is in it. I know the incoming senior class got their class pins and rings this week. In the box that he gives me is his class pin.

"I would like you to be my steady. I want to pin you."

I, of course, say yes. He momentarily takes the class pin out of the box, looks at the top of my dress, and tries to figure out where to place the pin. The shoulder strap is wide enough to hold the hook. He pushes the pin through the strap, and he adds the clasp. When he finished putting the pin in place, the top of his hand lay on my breast. I take my hand and gently put it on top of his, and we stay that way for a moment. He withdraws his hand from under mine, and we kiss.

I lean over. "I think we should go back inside."

We dance the rest of the night, and he takes me home when the prom is over. We sit in the car, kiss, and touch each other. What we are doing is taking place all over Waterloo that night.

Life Lessons Learned:

Signs and symbols are a way to send silent messages to people, and while I didn't know it that night, in the future, I would put my nurse's pin on someone significant to me.

At the prom, the dress my mother made was the envy of all the girls and women chaperones in the room. Only some people can be the center of attention. It is important to be humble if you are in the spotlight. At some point in your life, you will be in a room with somebody more important than you. How you handle that situation will go a long way to determining who you are.

CHAPTER 17:

School's Out, and a Great Summer Is Ahead

It takes me a few days to come down from the emotional high of the prom. I must refocus my attention on final exams. My school has a policy that you are exempt from taking a final exam if you maintain an A average throughout the year. I want to ensure that my final grade will not be impacted by not taking the final. I don't want to know that I will get a zero score for the last test even though I don't have to take the final. It would bring down my grade point average if counted as a zero.

I go to my homeroom teacher, Mrs. Williams, and ask, "Is it true that if I maintain an A average throughout the year, I don't have to take the final exam?"

"It is true, but to be safe, you should ask each of your teachers if you have to take their final."

I check with all my teachers and do not have to take any finals.

I went to school the last week and spent my time in the library reviewing the admittance applications for the two nursing schools. I continue my work at the hospital, but I have little time for John. We talk about how we are going to spend the summer. We agree we should spend some time at the lake and work on our tans. My problem is that my skin is so fair that I sunburn easily. I use a great deal of lotion. John says he thinks I use a lot of the lotion so I can slide out of his arms quickly.

Through the end of June, I continue to work in admissions at the hospital. Before the 4th of July, Miss Martin asks me to come in a little early the day after the 4th to talk about my next assignment.

John and I go to the town's annual firework display. We take a blanket and move to a less populated park. We put the blanket on the ground, lay on it, and wait for the fireworks to start.

While waiting, we are on our backs, and John turns on his side. He gently leans into me and gives me what I think is the best kiss he has ever given me. It is so powerful that it literally takes my breath away. I realize that in John's effort to get to my lips, his chest is putting pressure on my chest, limiting my ability to breathe. When our lip's part, John moves back, and I take a massive gulp of air.

"You were crushing me. I couldn't breathe, and I started to feel woozy."

Shortly after regaining my breath, the fireworks start. The 4th of July is one of my favorite holidays. I love fireworks. John and I attend the town parade with the marching units and veterans. This year's parade is special to me because one of the men marching is a veteran I met during my visit to the VA hospital.

My favorite fireworks are the ones that have blasts so powerful you can feel them in your chest. Sometimes the explosions are so loud that I am startled into John's arms, or so I tell him. After the fireworks are over, the townspeople start to leave the park and head home. We stay, and when everyone has gone, we play on the blanket, exploring each other, and then an alarm goes off in my brain. We have gone far enough. It is time to leave. As we walk home, we decide to have a picnic dinner by the lake in the woods off Myrtle Ave. before the summer is over.

We arrived at my house, and he didn't kiss me goodnight right away. He takes me in his arms and holds me gently. He opens his arms and lets me loose. Just before I escape, he pulls me back into his arms and gives me a soft goodnight kiss.

Life Lessons Learned:

I had accomplished something that a few people in the history of Our Lady of Victory's school had ever accomplished. I did not have to take any of my final exams. I had worked hard. I knew that the path to success came with hard work. In three months, I would have to start all over again. Life is a series of challenges that, once they are met, new ones confront us. One accurate measure of our success is how we accept the challenges. As an ER nurse, I believe I could simultaneously face many challenges. I would like to know if I can handle them.

CHAPTER 18:

New Assignment

I went to the hospital early because Miss Martin told me I would get a new assignment this week. I arrive at 2:30. I no longer must stop at the front desk. I go directly to her office. I knock on her door.

She says, "Come in."

I go in and say, "Good afternoon."

She says, "Miss Murphy, if I'm going to help you understand what it means to be a nurse, I must expose you to things other than medical information. One of the most important skills in being a great nurse is communicating with all kinds of people. I primarily put you in admissions to see how you interacted with people. The report back from admissions was that you did well on that assignment. Your next assignment will help you sharpen your communication skills. As you deliver incoming patients to their room, you may have seen a volunteer pushing a cart with many things that could be bought?"

"Yes, I noticed that cart. How will that help me be a better nurse?"

"As a nurse, you must gain patients' trust when caring for them. They will tell you how they feel so you can watch their progress. In this assignment, you will go to every room you can, which is essential to learn to interact immediately with the patient. Some people will talk with you during your rounds, and others appear stone-cold to you.

"You will learn the most from those who respond slowly. This assignment will also help you develop your power of observation. How someone speaks is a sign. You will also look for messages not spoken; body language. These signs and more will help you develop your communication skills. When you finish your day, stop by, and we will review what happened and what you learned today.

"You will find the cart in the gift shop, and you'll look for Mrs. Williams and introduce yourself. Tell her you will be taking over this shift. As you run out of things, you must return to the gift shop, turn in your receipts, and restock your cart. Any questions?"

I nodded no.

"Good luck and have a great shift. I'll see you at six."

I pull out my map and find the gift shop. I head straight for it. When I get there, I ask for Mrs. Williams. She is behind the counter checking out a customer with a purchase.

She says, "I'm Mrs. Williams, and I'll be right with you."

After she completes the sale, she comes around the counter, extends her hands, and asks me my name.

"I'm Mary Ellen Murphy, and I'm here to handle the cart for the rooms."

"Excellent. Let me show you where we keep the cart. You may have to come back during your shift to restock it, and at the end of your shift, it's your responsibility to restock it for the next person who takes over the cart."

"Got it. Where should I go first?"

"Miss Murphy, I suggest starting on the second floor with the general patients. It would be best if you had something on the cart for anybody who wants to buy something, either as a patient or for a patient. All the items have a price. The cart has a charge slip for you to write on the patient's name, room number, and bed if they share a room. Bring the charge slips to me, or whoever runs the register at your shift's end. Are you ready to get started?"

"Yes, ma'am."

I take the cart out of the storage room, and we check to ensure it's complete. I'm on my way. I get into the elevator, which is on the ground floor, and push button number 1. As I ride on the elevator, I realize that Mrs. Williams didn't tell me where I was supposed to start. I look down the hallway, and I see a nurse's station. I push my cart down to the station and introduce myself to one of the nurses.

"This is my first day working in the cart. Where do I start?"

The nurse looks up from the chart that she's working on.

"Welcome, Miss Murphy. People generally start at the far end of the hall with the lowest-numbered rooms first and then go up the hallway to the highest-numbered rooms."

"Should I knock on the door? If the door is open, do I walk in? What should I do?" I may be coming across as a little panicked.

"It would always be a good idea to knock, even if the door is open. I'd peek in to see if the patient is awake or asleep. If they're awake, then knock on the door and introduce yourself. Ask the patient if they need anything from the cart. When you're finished in one room, go to the next until you complete the hallway. If you have time left in your shift, go to floor two. The rest is up to you. Good luck."

Life Lessons Learned:

Always remember the value of an assignment. We can learn much, even with what we think is beneath us. Take every task with excitement about doing something different. You never know who you might run into. Anyone could be an important connection later in your life.

CHAPTER 19:

Ethel Smith

I take my cart and go down to the end of the hallway to room 101 and knock on the door. The room has two beds but only one occupant. I am nervous, but I must make my first visit. I see the chart at the foot of the bed with Ethel Smith's name on it.

"Good afternoon, Mrs. Smith. My name is Mary Ellen Murphy. You can buy things from the gift shop right off the cart. Is there anything you need?"

"Get the hell out of my room!"

To say I am shocked would be an understatement. I know I am young, but I have never had anybody yell and curse at me. Well, that's not entirely true. The basketball coach can yell and curse. So, I immediately apologized to Mrs. Smith and tried to find out what I did wrong.

I asked her, "Did I offend you somehow?"

"Yes, by being in my room! Would you please leave now?"

Whatever confidence I had is now totally shot. I start towards my cart to leave her alone and go to another room, but I turn around and go back to her.

"Mrs. Smith, I am a volunteer at this hospital. I don't get paid for the work that I do. I might like to become a nurse. Working in this hospital will give me experience and help me decide. I don't believe I've done anything that warrants your treatment of me. I want to do the best I can for you. I want to make your stay in this hospital as pleasant as possible. If the best way is for me to leave you alone, I will. I will not bother you anymore. I will take my cart and leave. I will advise the next volunteer not to bother you as long as you're here. I will ask her to forward your information to the other volunteers when they come on duty."

I turn to walk out the door when I hear her say, "My husband was killed in World War I. They never brought his body home."

I stop in my tracks and don't know what to do. I turn around and walk over to her bed. I told her something that I had heard my father say many times. It instilled in me pride in veterans and their families. "As difficult as it must be for you, I want to thank you for giving your husband to the service of our country. I am truly sorry that you and other wives, lovers, friends, and relatives experienced the same thing."

I can see her eyes welling up with tears. I have nothing else to say, so I turn again to leave the room.

I hear in a different tone, "Can you stay for a moment?"

I turn, go back, and sit by her bed. I take her hand and gently hold it. "Would you like me to arrange for a priest to come and pray with you?"

"No, but would you pray with me?"

I say, "Of course."

We pray the Our Father together, and when we finish, we are both quiet.

I stand up and say, "I have some other people to visit, but I'll stop by on my way home to see how you're doing. I'm here three to four days a week, so I'll look for an opportunity to stop in and see how you're doing each day. And you know what? I'm going to have Father Murphy stop to say hello."

I walk towards the door, but before I leave, I turn back and ensure she can see me. I wave to her and smile, and she smiles and waves back.

Life Lessons Learned:

I learned a vital lesson with my first patient, Mrs. Smith. When confronted with a challenge, do we take it on or abandon it for something more manageable? Do we turn the challenge over to somebody else because we want to avoid doing it? That was the decision I had to make. I could have walked out the door and pushed my cart to the next room. Nobody would have criticized me for doing that, because the nurses on the floor knew that Mrs. Smith was hard to deal with. Over my nursing career, I have had many Mrs. and Mr. Smiths looking for compassion. That day, I may not have had training to be a nurse, but I passed my first test.

Room 101 at St. Mary's Hospital helped mature me that day. Ethel Smith just needed someone to share her grief. I took the time to stop and listen, as opposed to just walking away.

CHAPTER 20:

My Father Calls a Meeting

When I came home from the hospital, my father was in the kitchen and said, "I need you to eat as soon as possible because we have to have a family meeting." I don't know if it is because it is Friday the 13th or because my father feels the need to share a concern with all of us, but we don't have much warning like we usually do for a family meeting. He told my mother, brother, and sister before I got home. I eat as quickly as possible and put my dishes in the sink. He sees me put the dishes in the sink and tells everybody, "Let's go to the dining room."

We all sit down, and he says, "I must share a couple of concerns with you that I have been thinking and reading about for some time. One just happened today. As you know, we are in what is being called the Roaring '20s, which means that times are good, and people are spending money with little concern for savings. They buy cars and clothes and live for today with very little thought about the future. People are taking their life savings and getting house mortgages to put money in the stock market.

"It seems easy to make money in the markets. People are not concerned about the risk and only focus on potential profits. I decided today to sell all the stocks I have in our investments."

We don't know how much money Father has, but when he decides to take all the money that he has out of the market, we know that is very important.

"I told all of you some time ago that your mother and I believe that the most important thing we can do for you is provide you with a good education. I've taken all the money from the investments and a substantial portion of the money in the bank and bought U.S. government bonds. I share this information with you, but I must insist that you promise your most solemn promise that you will not disclose what I say to anybody. Do I have your promise?"

We all can tell Father is serious. We agree we won't tell anybody. I tell my father I will not even tell John.

"The second concern I want to discuss also happened today, and it confirms to me the correctness of my decision and brings home to me what I've been reading and hearing for months."

We have no idea what Father is going to say. We are all in our seats, waiting for him to tell us.

"I stopped at the filling station on my way home from work. A young man was pumping the gas. He said to me, 'Are you interested in stocks? Everybody's interested in stocks. I'm investing in the market, and I'm going to make a lot of money. I won't be pumping gas much longer.' Then he said, 'If you want, I can give you a tip on a stock to buy.' I was stunned. I asked him, 'How old are you, young man?' He responded that he was twenty-one. I was flabbergasted at his response. I wondered if the whole country had gone crazy. Was I doing something wrong by not speculating on stocks?

"I concluded that I could be wrong and lose it all. I heard from other people putting all their savings in the stock market. I couldn't risk my children's future. Only time will tell whether I made the right decision or not. I do know I haven't put your college money at risk. Do you have any questions?"

We are all silent for a moment.

Kelly asks the first question: "How bad do you think it could get, Dad?"

He thinks for a moment, then responds, "Kelly, let me put it this way. Let's say we have a 12-inch diameter balloon and keep putting air in it. It swells to 15 inches. It will eventually burst if we keep putting more air in the balloon. The other possibility is that an over-inflated balloon will begin to develop a leak. No matter how much air you try to pump into the balloon, it continues to get smaller and smaller and smaller. I don't know how much longer this speculation can last. I don't think it will be a slow leak. I think it'll be a major explosion like the over-inflated balloon."

I look at my father and say, "You and Mom know that I want to go to nursing school. Are you telling us you set aside money to pay for college? If it gets as bad as you think, will the colleges still be in business?"

"Fortunately for you, we will still need nurses. If we see a significant downturn, it would be a good idea to keep in touch with the school regularly."

My brother asks, "Will we have enough food?"

"Patrick, that is a great question. You know that garden we have out back? We will all pitch in and double the garden size so we can grow as much food as possible. Your mother and I have talked about these things. We think we may have more meetings if things get bad. We love all of you, and we will do whatever we need to keep you safe."

Life Lessons Learned:

I learned from my father that day to plan for the worst and hope for the best. I learned it was also essential to educate yourself about what was happening around you. We must make decisions about ourselves and others to do our best.

CHAPTER 21:

My Future in a Big Envelope

A phone sits on the table by the front door of our house. The table is large enough to have a chair underneath it to sit on when we're making a phone call. The top of the desk is also where Mom places mail addressed to any children.

Things are different today. While I was working at the hospital, my mom put an envelope on the kitchen table in front of my plate.

When I got home, my mom said that I had some mail, and I asked if she knew who it was from. She didn't answer. I go through the kitchen to the front room, where the correspondence is usually kept, but my mom says, "It's by your plate."

I run back to the kitchen, where I see a large envelope on the table. I don't sit down to open it, but I see on the outside that it is from St. Joseph's School of Nursing in Chicago, Illinois. Instantly, my heart starts beating very fast. My pulse is racing like running one of my basketball coach's line-to-line sprints.

I sit down and open the envelope. I take out the contents: a series of brochures and a cover letter. The letter is from Sister Mary Elizabeth, OP, who is the school's president. Her letter says, in part, "Thank you for writing to me. I have enclosed brochures showing where you will live and what you will study if you come to St. Joseph's. I want to invite you to come and spend a weekend. I want you to learn about the school. If you wish to come for a visit, I will need some notice in advance. I hope you can come and visit our excellent school. You need to see if it's a fit for you. I look forward to hearing from you."

I hand the letter to my mother and look at the brochures. In my letter to the school, I asked for two copies of all the brochures. I want a set for me and one for my parents. That is precisely what the school has sent to me. I separate all the flyers into two stacks. I give one set to my mother.

She goes to the stove, takes my dinner plate out of the oven, and puts it in front of me. Then, she sits down next to me and tells me to eat. "You can go through the brochures later."

"I can do both. I can look at the brochures and eat at the same time."

My mother laughs and says, "Okay."

The brochures are just as sister said — one is about the school, one is about the curriculum, and the last is about campus life.

Also, Sister Elizabeth includes two applications — one for the school and one for a scholarship. I set both of those aside. I put the brochures down on the table. I quickly gobble down my dinner. I eat so fast that my mom says, "Slow down or you'll choke."

I slow down but am anxious to see what the brochures say, so I wolf down the rest of the food and drink a good-sized glass of water.

My mom takes my plate and puts it in the sink. "You come back and sit next to me."

Together, we start to go through the brochures.

We both go quickly through all the brochures. Mom looks at the curriculum. I look at campus life.

Life Lessons Learned:

Information is essential when beginning a new chapter of your life. When I made the decision that I wanted to leave Waterloo, I knew nothing of the world outside of my hometown. I started off trying to decide without a significant amount of information. My friend in the library gave me some data on being a nurse and what the educational requirement would be in a School of Nursing. But what about where I was going to live? What is the city or town like?

I made the decision that I had to go and see it for myself. If you have an opportunity for a new job and must leave your hometown, you must see what it offers.

In this time of depression, people are forced to leave their homes and go anywhere to find work so the family can survive. They strike out not knowing if they will find work; they know they can no longer stay where they are. In many cases, they leave their roots where their family has been for generations. It's hard to leave your hometown regardless of whether you want to or must.

CHAPTER 22:

I May Not Go Home for Three Years

I focus on the brochure for student life. Before I got the brochure, I knew very little about nursing schools. As I read the material, the romance of being a nurse is losing some of its luster as the practical reality of what it takes sinks in. The program is three years long. You go year-round with no summers off. I would only get two weeks off in August.

I would attend classes like a regular college and spend many hours in the hospital beside a trained nurse, helping take care of patients. I would work most weekends. The idea of partying in downtown Chicago over the weekends will be challenging. It seems like much work, but there is a lot to learn, and three years is a little time.

The brochure has a picture and a line drawing of the dormitory room. It is very similar to the room I share with Kelly, but the dorm room is more significant than my space with Kelly. I would have one roommate, so my experience living with my big sister would make the transition to living with a roommate a lot easier.

They show pictures of the school, the hospital, and the surroundings, all of which look modern and well-kept. I notice one of the pictures is of their gymnasium. I see basketball hoops. The next part of the brochure talks about the cost. This is what surprises me, at least initially. I would be going year-round with two weeks off, and the price is for room and board at about a dollar a day. Initially, I couldn't figure out why it was so cheap. I read on, and the reason becomes more evident in the details.

The brochure says that students must work in the hospital in the evenings during the week and on weekends in exchange for their tuition. It also points out that all graduates would be offered a paid position working in the hospital as a nursing assistant while they are preparing for the nursing exam. Once the student passes the exam, they become a registered nurse and are immediately offered a job at the hospital. They are also free to look at other hospitals for employment. With their certificate and education at a prestigious nursing school, they could find a job anywhere in the country.

There is a small paragraph that says students can apply for a scholarship. It indicates that there are few scholarships. Financial aid could be available for the right student. The average incoming class is 40 nurses, but at the end of the three-year period, only 25 to 30 will actually graduate.

I want to look at the curriculum, and I will get there. I stop momentarily and ask myself what I think of the time commitment. Now, I have some essential questions.

Do I want to leave Waterloo and my family, ostensibly for three years right after high school? I am close to my parents, my sister, and my brother. The idea of abruptly leaving everybody I know and not being able to see them for months at a time, or perhaps longer, is a terrifying thought for me.

I wonder about all my friends here in Waterloo. What about my boyfriend, John? It is then that I realize that after this school year, I will still have my senior year, but John will be off to college. We will be separated, and if he comes back to Waterloo, I most likely will not be there.

John and I are going to have to talk about this soon.

Life Lessons Learned:

If we pay attention to the small decisions in life, when it comes time to make a big one, we have some training. The more decisions we make build our confidence to make the next one.

CHAPTER 23:

What Will It Cost? Can We Afford It?

My mother and I exchange papers. I give her my student life package, and she gives me fees, charges, and curriculum. I am interested in the curriculum, but what it will cost is third in my priorities. Based on what I can see, the cost for the school would be about a dollar a day, or $30 a month. That money is used to pay for room and board, not the educational experience. I need to check this with one of the nurses at the hospital who went to St. Joseph's to make sure I've got it right. I find out that the $30 is for the whole year. The result is that the tuition, room, and board expense is $90 for three years.

For now, we pay room and board $30 per year. The educational experience is paid for when I spend evenings and weekends working in the hospital. Nursing school is almost free to me. The brochure also says a scholarship is possible to purchase books, clothes, transportation, and social activities. I would ask about that on my school visit.

I must find out from my dad and mom how much they can afford to pay, and my conversation with the former student should give me some idea of a better number of what it would cost me to attend. I set that aside and tell my parents we should talk, but I want to find out from a former student how much the extra expenses will be before we have a serious discussion.

Next, on to the subject matter to be taught. I have never felt so inadequate. I am going into my junior year. I have never heard of some of the subjects. I doubt I will see them for the remainder of my time in high school. Sitting down with my biology teacher and reviewing the subject matter is a good idea. I need to find out what she thinks about my ability to succeed.

The first year's subjects are anatomy, psychology, chemistry, bacteriology, drugs and solutions, nutrition, cookery, personal hygiene, ethics and nursing principles of medicine, nursing and medicine, tuberculosis massage, and diet and disease. The most extensive time consumer in my first year is the principles and practices of elementary nursing. I am expected to complete 652 hours of learning.

On the surface, it is few hours — only 13 hours a week. I must add to that working in the hospital during nights and weekends. Based on my estimate, I may spend as many as 35 hours a week working in the hospital. I need to check with my nursing friend if my numbers are close to reality. The subject matter is clearly more difficult than I expected. How many hours of study would be necessary for each course?

I put the curriculum brochure down because I am beginning to feel overcome. I am concerned that I'm not smart enough for nursing school. Graduating from high school and trying to find a good man to marry may not be such a bad idea after all. If I don't attend nursing school, I will be here when John comes home from college. We can spend time together and lay the foundation for our relationship. I like the way that sounds. I am giving up my dream because it will be hard to accomplish. I should settle for Waterloo.

I have many things to do. School starts next week, so John and I will picnic on the lake tomorrow night. That's more important to think about than anything else.

I buy a new bathing suit that is just gorgeous. It's almost skintight, and I think John will really like me in it. I'm going to tell Mom that I'm still studying the brochures. I have some things I need to get more information on from a college graduate nurse. I will share it with her and Dad as soon as I can.

Life Lessons Learned:

If success was easy, then the work to get it would be easy. But it's not. If you want to grow, you must challenge yourself. You can't give up your goal because the work to achieve the goal is challenging.

CHAPTER 24:

The Picnic and More on the Lake

I put together an ensemble for the picnic on the lake. I bought a beautiful bathing suit in pure white designed to fit my figure. The saleslady suggests we attach a strap on each side of the back to secure the suit around my body.

She says, "You don't want anything slipping out if you plan to be active on the beach."

It has straps at the top; they go around my neck and tie in the back.

I find a pair of moderate-length shorts in tan-colored fabric. The shorts have a neat-looking cuff of about one inch. I go across the street from Smith's Department Store to the thrift store and find an old woven belt that is too long for me. I am going to let the excess strap hang down. Next, I find a man's white dress shirt with long, well-worn sleeves. I like the look. And finally, I see an old man's fedora-felt hat. The hat is tan, so it matches the shorts and the belt. My outfit is complete.

My mother makes some fried chicken and potato salad for us. We put them in containers in a picnic basket along with giant oatmeal raisin cookies. John is responsible for bringing a galvanized bucket with half a dozen bottles of Coca-Cola on ice. As I am getting dressed, I look at each piece as I put it on to see if I still like the look. I look very sophisticated. My sister thinks it is a striking combination. She wants to know if she can borrow it for a date with her boyfriend.

I said, "Of course, you can. I'll let you know how things turn out."

John picks me up at 6:30. We take a large blanket, beach towels, and pillows. It seems like a lot of stuff to just go and make out. John will bring some newspapers to start a fire and gather some wood. We aren't cooking anything, but I think the fire will be romantic. I don't know for sure what is going to happen tonight. I am prepared to say yes or no if sex comes up. I can't believe I seriously think John and I might have sex.

Promptly at 6:30, John knocks on the door.

My mother says, "Come on in. She's almost ready."

I come downstairs, and John says, "Wow, you look terrific."

"Thank you. Let's go."

We walk out the front door carrying our stuff. We head to the pond at the end of Myrtle Street. John tells me he went there earlier in the day and found the perfect spot. He cleaned it up and stacked some firewood. It is ready to go. I can tell he is excited about the evening, and so am I, but we are both a little nervous.

It doesn't take long to drive to the woods and get to John's selected site. We set up our spot and decide to go into the lake and cool down for many reasons — mainly because it is a hot night.

We get in and swim for a while. We embrace and kiss for the longest time. Our bodies touch each other. That spark that has been growing throughout the summer is blazing tonight. The lake's calm water doesn't cool us down as I hoped it would. The fabric of my bathing suit is relatively thin. John has no shirt on, so our contact is excellent. When we separate, I notice John staring intently at my chest. The thin fabric can't hide my nipples. Initially, I was embarrassed. I try to cover them up. John pulls me close.

John suggests we return to our blanket and get ready for dinner. We dry off, lay on the blanket, put the pillows under our heads, and watch the sunset. I am in his arms, and we don't say much. On the spur of the moment, I roll over on top of John. He puts his arms around me. We kiss again.

I am stroking his hair, still damp from being in the lake. John drops his hands gently on my behind. He starts rubbing it gently. Several times he slips his fingers under the edge of the bathing suit then pulls them out. He continues to gently work his way up my spine to my shoulders and my hair. The heat generated by our passion makes the night air seem even heavier. He drops his hands to the middle of my back and unties the strap. I know what he is doing. I don't stop him. I don't object. Once the belt is undone, he moves his hands from my waist to my neck.

After a little while, he reaches up and unties the strap around my neck. He has a strap in each hand, and we both know if I rise, the top of my bathing suit will come down, and my breasts will be exposed. I say as much to John.

"Is that what you want? Or do you want even more?"

"You are a beautiful woman. I have strong feelings for you. I hope you do for me, so the answer is yes. I would like to see them, touch them, hold them, kiss them. Of course, I would like more, but only if you want it too. I brought the condoms if you think you're ready to use them."

I am facing the most significant decision that I've faced in my life. If I rise, the flame of passion could also rise rapidly. I am not sure either of us can control it. Part of me wants him to see me. I must decide. I put my hands on John's shoulders and slowly push the upper part of my body up. I can see the excitement in his eyes, and I know that it will continue. I reach the point where the top of the bathing suit is down far enough that the momentum of gravity will push my breasts out and onto John's chest.

He lets go of the straps and looks at me. He waits for the longest time. He is just staring at what has just been exposed to him. I feel strange. I don't rush to pull up the bathing suit. I watch him look at my breasts in amazement. After a while, John puts his arms around me and draws me close. We are together skin to skin. I must admit it is a fantastic feeling.

As I lay half-naked in his arms, a thought comes over me like a tidal wave. John has a condom. We can both get naked and have sex tonight and see where that leads us. If I have sex with John tonight, I've confirmed my thoughts this afternoon that I am not smart enough to attend nursing school. Would I be better off if we have a sexual relationship and see if he continues that relationship after college? Do I get married with three kids, living in Waterloo, Iowa?

No, I don't want to do this. I want to be a nurse. At that moment, I put my hands on his shoulders and pushed myself straight up. I don't care that I am exposed. I am looking down at John, and I am going to tell him what is going to happen going forward.

"We should get dressed and have something to eat. Then we'll talk about the future."

I am not embarrassed that I am naked. I am thrilled that he was impressed with my naked body. I decide I will not sacrifice my future for sex tonight. I get dressed. John ties my straps. We sit on the blanket, eat chicken and potato salad, and drink ice-cold Coca-Cola.

We sit on the blanket for the longest time, and then with a smile, John says, "Those are magnificent. Thanks for allowing me to see them."

We both laugh.

Life Lessons Learned:

That night, a 17-year-old girl, half-naked on a blanket beside a lake on a romantic evening, became a determined woman. When we are young, our passions can significantly influence our decisions. Sometimes those decisions, which at the time seem to be so right, can be wrong.

CHAPTER 25:

Back to School

My junior year in high school is the scariest for me, my family, the people of Waterloo, and the whole nation. I have been at school for about a month when the news comes out that the stock market is falling.

Many people with the bulk of their savings in the stock market lose it overnight. They are destitute. People lose their jobs, their houses, and are homeless. They call it the "Great Depression." There is nothing remarkable about it.

My father proves wise by taking almost all his money out of the stock market and buying U.S. government bonds. At his job, his hours are cut, but he still has a job. My mother also keeps her career because of her skill. Her hours at the store are reduced. I continue to volunteer at the hospital, and I transfer from department to department, learning as much as possible. I am trying to get the highest scores on my schoolwork, even as I continue volunteering. Every day that I go to the hospital, I am more convinced that I want to be a nurse.

I need to do everything on my checklist to get answers before my mother and father decide if they can afford to send me to nursing school. My father finally said today that I don't have to get a scholarship. They can pay, but a scholarship would help pay for other college expenses like uniforms, shoes, and stockings.

In a meeting with my parents, I ask them, "Can we go to Chicago and look at the school?"

My father indicates that he's already looked at the map. He tells me that, depending upon driving conditions, it will take us the better part of a day to get there. We will spend a day at the school and take a day to get back home.

My father asks me to write to the school to find out when we can visit. Dad says he will look at the train schedule as a possible option for getting there. He will let us know, but it may just be Mom and me going to Chicago because of the cost. I hope Dad can work it out so all three of us can see the school.

It is the end of October, and things have settled in the country. We might have already gotten through the worst part of the decline.

Before Thanksgiving, I received a letter from the school saying we have an appointment on Friday, December 6. I sit down with my mom and dad to talk about the letter. Dad says we can all go. I am thrilled, so I count the days until we pack up the car and drive to Chicago.

I will start the next phase of my life in a big city. While in Chicago, John gets his acceptance letter from the University of Pennsylvania School of Engineering. We have a lot to talk about when I get back from Chicago.

For the rest of the year and into the spring of 1930, John and I spend much time together. Sometimes my blouse gets wrinkled on both sides. He never presses me for sex and doesn't look for a new girlfriend.

After the Christmas season of 1929, our discussions turned to him going away to college and our separation. I tell him we are friends, not lovers, and he should make new friends in college. I would be happy to see him when he returns home for breaks. If I go to nursing school, there is a good chance, except for two weeks in the summer, that I will not see him for three years.

Life Lessons Learned:

To this day, I have never forgotten that hot August evening on the blanket by the lake. John and I remained friends for years after. We both left Waterloo for good. His wife, Helen, sent me a note telling me he had been killed in the war. He was such a nice man. I felt sorry the world didn't benefit from what he could've contributed.

The day will come when someone near and dear to you will die. Life is about living, but when you experience death for the first time, it can be more dramatic than all the other deaths you experience. If the death is tied to someone you loved and were close to, it's even more devastating.

As an ER nurse over the years, I witnessed death many times. Sometimes people come into your life for a short period, and they make a strong and lasting impression. We don't know why, but they do, and when they die, it is an impression that we carry with us the rest of our lives.

CHAPTER 26:

St. James Hospital, School of Nursing in Chicago

My room at the St. James Hotel is fabulous. It is the first time I have a room of my own. As great as the room is, I cannot get to sleep. At 3 a.m., I make a mistake.

I go to the window, pull back the curtain, and look outside. I expect the world outside to be dark. From my room, I can see the skyline of downtown Chicago. My view is mesmerizing. I can see many buildings, some 400 to 500 feet tall. The tallest building in Chicago is under construction. The Chicago Board of Trade building is supposed to tower over 600 feet into the sky.

I fall asleep on the window seat, looking at the skyline. I hear a *thump, thump* coming from somewhere. I stand up and walk towards the noise from the adjoining doors between my room and my parent's. I open it, and my mother and father are fully dressed, waiting for me.

I quickly ask, "What time is it?"

My mother responds, "It is 7 a.m."

I am still in my pajamas. I know we have an appointment at 9 o'clock.

My father says, "You've got plenty of time. Try out that shower. When you are ready, we will go have breakfast."

The shower is amazing. The night before, I had taken a long hot shower before I put on my pajamas and got into bed. Now I am going to have a chance to take another shower. This time, I don't linger. I want to get something to eat before we leave for the school.

My clothes are laid out from the night before. I know exactly what I am going to wear. I linger just a little more in the shower. I step out, dry myself off, comb my hair, dress, and am ready to go.

I knock on my parents' door and ask, "Ready?"

We go down to the coffee shop and have a hearty breakfast. My father called down for the car to be ready after breakfast.

The doorman says, "Your car is here. Do you know where you're going?"

"Yes, we drove there last night, thank you."

As soon as the car door slams, I know my life will change forever. Nothing much is said in the car. With plenty of time to spare, we arrive at the school. We go to the parking lot that we found last night. We walk over to the school's front door and slowly up the steps. We go through the massive brass doors. Inside we see a desk that says, "Information."

I walk over to the nun behind the desk, and she asks if we have an appointment.

"Yes, for 9 o'clock." I turn and see a clock on the wall. It is 8:40. "I realize we're a little early, but I didn't want to be late."

"I will tell Sister that you're here."

Promptly at 9 a.m., Sister Mary Francis comes through the door. She walks over to us.

"Is this the Murphy family?"

My father answers, "Yes," and introduces my mother and me.

"Wonderful to meet you. Please follow me. We're going to a conference room to talk about the school."

A pot of coffee, juice, and a pastry is on a credenza in the room. Sister Mary Francis says, "Please help yourself."

She takes a cup of coffee with cream and sugar and sits at the table. We join her at the table with our beverages and pastry.

"Again, I want to welcome you to our school. I want to talk a bit about what we will accomplish today. I will try and answer all your questions. If, by chance, I don't know the answer, I will get it to you before you leave today."

She passes a folder to each of us and encourages us to open it. In it are many of the same brochures we reviewed before.

Sister starts speaking: "We are a diploma institution. You will get a diploma if you complete all the requirements within three years. It certifies that you have completed the required coursework successfully. Your next step will be to take the license exam. It is generally taken within three months after your graduation.

"The school is home to 50 first-year students. In the second and third years, we will have less than 50 students in each class. The attrition rate in the first year is around 20%, or 10 students. The curriculum is challenging and requires a great deal of work to keep up. Students who cannot keep up cannot stay here. If you graduate, you are assured of having a nursing position at St. James Hospital upon graduation.

"One other thing... The price to attend the school includes your room and board, tuition, fees, uniforms, and books. All incoming first-year students have individual rooms. Second and third-year students share a room with another nurse candidate. The cost for the three-year program is $90. You pay for it by the year. We keep the cost as low as possible. The student must help in the hospital at least three evenings a week and work one eight-hour shift on Saturday and Sunday. Finally, you will have two weeks off per year in August. If you want to go home on the weekend to visit family, you must ensure your shifts are covered at the hospital.

"If, for some reason upon graduation, you do not wish to work at St. James Hospital, you are free to look for other employment. I am confident that our graduates are in significant demand. We will have a morning tour of some of the facilities, including classrooms and dormitories, and then lunch. Then, I will take you on a tour of the hospital. Finally, you can meet some of your potential teachers."

Sister has been speaking for an hour. I sit on the edge of my seat, listening to every word she says. When she finishes, she asks, "Do you have any questions so far?"

All three of us ask several questions, and there isn't anything that sister can't answer. When we are finished asking our questions, Sister asks, "Would you like to see where you're going to live when you come here?"

I say, "Yes, Sister, but I need to use the restroom first."

We go out in the hallway, and Sister shows me the restroom. I go in not only because I must go to the bathroom, but also because I want to be alone. I need to be in a private place where I can say, "Yes, this is where I want to be!"

Life Lessons Learned:

Growing up, my parents provided everything – house, food, clothing, education, love, and encouragement. It isn't until I am about to leave home and must ask my parents for money to begin the next part of my life that I realize how dependent I am on them.

It's tough because my family doesn't have many resources to be able to afford the expense of college. I am glad they are willing to spend whatever they can to give me the opportunity they think I deserve. I understand my parents' sacrifice for me to have what I want.

A part of me doesn't want to ask my parents to send me to nursing school. I understand it would not have been possible without their support.

Our nation's history has been that each generation wants the next generation to be better than the previous one. Parents with no college education take great pride in being able to help their children get the best education they can. As we grow up and away from our families and have our own children, we also want them to have a better life.

CHAPTER 27:

This is Going to be Hard

I like my dorm room. It is bigger than the room I share with Kelly. It has a bed, a desk with a light, a chair, a dresser, and a closet. I ask Sister if I can see what the shared rooms look like. We stop by and look at the two-person room.

It is bigger than the one-person room, but with two beds, it seems smaller. From there, we look at the rest of the grounds. There are plenty of spaces to sit and study in the fresh air. It has a small gymnasium with two basketball hoops. I am excited to see that, and Sister asks, "Do you play basketball?"

"Yes," my father says, "And she's good at it."

From there, we go to lunch. After lunch, we meet some teachers and talk about complicated coursework. From there, we visit the hospital to look at the training facility. I will spend many hours learning the practical side of being a nurse. We go back to the conference room. There is coffee, tea, water, and cookies waiting for us. I have a cup of tea and three cookies. I take them over to the table and quickly eat them. My father asks some questions about payment.

He asks Sister, "Besides transportation and spending money, is there anything else we must pay for that hasn't been discussed?"

Sister replies that she is unaware of any additional expenses. Next, the conversation turns to academics.

"We are a very prestigious school of nursing, so many young women apply to our school. We take 50 first-year students and look for the best and brightest. The work is complex and challenging, and not everybody can excel. Miss Murphy, you are about to start your junior year of high school, correct?"

I respond, "Yes, Sister."

"We will need to see a transcript of your grades at the end of your junior year. The school will also want letters of recommendation from your biology teacher, the principal of the school, and one other reference letter from a person you choose. After we receive all your paperwork, the admissions committee will start reviewing the possibility of you coming to our school. If we decide that you are the kind of person we think can excel in nursing, we will issue you a letter of acceptance before Christmas of your senior year.

"You must decide and get back to us with a signed letter of intent by January 15. That letter of acceptance is conditional that the balance of your senior year will see a continuation of your academic achievements. Your time at St. James will commence on September 1 after your June graduation. You should expect to be here the last week of August so that you can get settled in your room. You will need time to get your books and find your way around the campus so that on the first day of school, you're ready to go and potentially become one of the best nurses in America."

I am reticent and say nothing. Sister asks if we have any additional questions.

My mother speaks. "Sister, I am a professional dressmaker. May I make uniforms for my daughter to wear to school?"

"That's an excellent question. Many girls don't believe that they can survive with just three uniforms. They will buy two more to have a fresh one each day. We use a McCall uniform pattern for the nurse's uniforms. If the uniforms look very similar to the ones you provide, we have no problem. If you want to make a couple of extra uniforms, that is fine by us. They do get a great deal of wear. You should expect to be making additional uniforms each year."

At that point, Sister asks if there are any more questions.

We all respond, "No, and thank you."

Sister walks us to the front door, turns to me, and says, "Miss Murphy, I hope we see you in the hallways of St. James."

We go out the door and back to the car. We drive back to the hotel. Not much is said in the car. I think we are overwhelmed with the school, the curriculum, and the challenges ahead of me.

When we get to our rooms, I tell my parents, "I'm exhausted. Do you mind if I lay down for a while?"

"We can have dinner a bit later and talk," my father says. "We'll see you soon."

I go into my room, remove my clothes, put on my luxurious hotel bathrobe, climb into bed, and pull the covers up to my chin. Try as much as I can, I can't fall asleep. The only thing I can think about is that this will be much harder than I thought. I continuously wonder if I am smart enough to do this.

Life Lessons Learned:

Not very often in our lives do we find ourselves facing life-changing decisions. Sometimes, they are complex and agonizing to make. Because they're so important, they demand a significant amount of thought. We must believe in ourselves and our capabilities before we make that decision.

Many times as a nurse, when I faced a critical, life-threatening situation, I drew more and more on my past life experiences, trying to find the wisdom to make the best possible decision for the patient.

CHAPTER 28:

Back to Waterloo

After we return to our hotel room from the school visit, I go to my room. My father goes downstairs and asks for directions to the nearest Catholic Church.

The man at the front desk says, "St. Patrick's Church is just down the street. It's an easy walk. Their first Mass is at 7:30."

After dinner, when we go to our rooms, Dad tells us that Mass is at 7:30, and he wants to leave the hotel at 7 o'clock. "After church, we will return for breakfast, pack the car, and head back to Waterloo."

I sleep the night snugly in my hotel robe. When I hear the knock on my door, I say, "Yes, Mom, I'm awake. I will be ready by seven."

The morning is crisp. We walk to church as we think about the trip home to Waterloo. The priest's sermon at Mass deals with Jesus's journey and how we also have a journey that will eventually take us to God. We are in control of what type of journey we will have. Will it be selfish, or will we have compassion for our fellow man in the difficult times we face as a nation and a world?

I realize that I've been so self-absorbed that I am not paying attention to what's happening all over our country, even in Waterloo, Iowa. When Mass is over, we return to the hotel and have breakfast. We don't say much at breakfast. I think we are all anxious to get in the car and head home. We meet in the lobby with our bags. The doorman has already brought the car to the front door. He and my father pack the bags. My father smiles and gives him a generous tip. We get in the car and are on our way to Waterloo.

There is minimal conversation in the car as we are leaving Chicago. When the Windy City is clearly behind us, my mother asks, "Have you thought about everything you need to do between now and June to file your application? Do you want to look at any other schools? Are you sure that being a nurse is what you want?"

I think about the serious questions she asks. I don't answer quickly. I want to try and respond as a responsible adult.

"I think I would like to look at the school in Iowa just for comparison. I'm convinced that being a nurse is a call from the Lord that I must listen to. I must ask the two of you the most important question. I have about six months before I file my formal application. Then, I will have more than a year before I start school. I do not know what will happen to this country. I do believe there'll always be a need for nurses. The most important decision is not one that I need to make. It is one that you must make. Can we afford the cost of school? If we can't, I would like to know as soon as possible so that I can try and find some kind of work to earn money for my schooling."

My father says, "Your mother and I have been talking regularly. We have enough savings to protect the family and pay for your schooling. I would like you to apply for scholarship money. If you can get it, we can set money aside for your trips home and two-week annual vacations."

I am so excited to hear what my father is saying. I shout in the car, "I can go to Chicago! I can't tell you how happy I am and how much I love both of you for what you're doing for me! I promise that I will make you proud of me and be the best nurse I can be."

Things go quiet in the car for a while. Then, the conversation picks up as we relive the best day of my life. I can tell that my parents are as excited as I am. Their daughter will be the first nurse in our family. I will be the first college-educated person in our family.

We stop for lunch and dinner on the way home. After a long drive, the car pulls into the driveway at 1575 Myrtle Ave. It is late at night. My sister and brother want to hear all about the trip. The three of us stay up way too late. My sister must go to work in the morning, and my brother must go to school. I am glad they take such a keen interest in the trip. They are part of what I am going to do.

Life Lessons Learned:

When the Lord gives you a gift, you must manage the gift to its fullest amount. Over my life, the Lord has given me many gifts. My greatest gifts are the members of my family who have supported and encouraged me to do His work. I have the responsibility to help other people recognize their gifts. I must encourage them to utilize their unique gifts to their fullest extent.

CHAPTER 29:

My First Test

The weekend after we leave Chicago is the annual Christmas tree hunt. In the past, the hunters were my father, older sister, and younger brother. This year is different. My sister must work that weekend, so I take her place. It is the first time that I ever take part in selecting a Christmas tree. There is a tree farm outside of Waterloo where you can cut down your Christmas tree at a very affordable price. The three of us get in the car with an ax, a saw, and a rope.

It takes us about 25 minutes to get to the farm. Because it is early on Saturday morning, there aren't many people there.

I ask my father, "What is the process? How do we find the right one?"

"We walk around and look at trees, knowing we need one fitting in the living room. It must have a nice shape. When we find a potential one, we all stand around it and judge it from different angles to decide if it is right. If we agree it's the one, we use the saw or the ax to cut it as close as possible to the ground. The rope ties it up to keep the branches from flopping around when we secure it to the top of the car. When we get home, I will put it in a bucket of water on the back porch. I'll set it up in the living room sometime over the next week, and we can decorate it."

We start looking, each going our way. I'm not a discerning Christmas tree buyer because they all look good. My father and brother are picky. I hear each of them shout, "I found it!" This means we must see their perfect trees.

We see Patrick's tree first, and then Dad's selection. I would've been happy with either one, but the experts talk about the fine points of both trees. After going back and forth several times and looking at both trees, the decision is that Patrick has selected the tree for the living room this year.

Patrick thinks he is old enough to cut down the tree alone. My father agrees and tells him that he should use the saw. He needs to cut it as close to the ground as possible. Patrick crawls under the tree with the saw. My father is holding up a branch for Patrick and Patrick starts sawing. I am not watching Patrick until I hear him scream, and then I look at him.

I can see blood on the ground. I quickly look under the tree to see what is wrong. Patrick says the saw slipped off the trunk and cut into his leg. He thinks it is deep. I can see that he is losing a lot of blood. The only thought that comes to mind is, "I must stop the bleeding."

I tell my father, "Hand me the rope and find me a strong twig."

He does both quickly. I wrap the rope around Patrick's leg about 6 inches above the cut to make a tourniquet with the twig to stop the bleeding. Dad gets the car to take Patrick to the hospital while I am working on Patrick. Because Dad can't get the car to Patrick, the two of us carry him, and I get in the backseat with him. I put his leg on my lap to elevate it. It takes about 20 minutes, with my father driving too fast to reach the emergency room.

Two doctors and three nurses come out to the car and help Patrick onto the gurney. They rush him into the emergency room, and my father and I wait for what seems like hours. The doctor comes out to give us a report on Patrick and asks my father, "Whose idea was the tourniquet?"

My father says, "My daughter, who's going to be a nurse."

The doctor turns to me and says, "Young lady, you probably saved your brother's leg. The saw cut deeply into his leg and part of the bone. We were able to repair the artery. The cut in the bone was not too deep so that it would repair itself over time. His leg will be as good as new."

I ask the doctor, "When can we see him?"

"He's still under anesthetic. I think in about two hours, you'll be able to see him."

My father and I thank the doctor for his good work. After the doctor leaves, my father puts his arms around me and thanks me for caring for my little brother. I am somewhat embarrassed about what happened, but I am also glad I could help my brother.

I say to my father, "We have quite a bit of time before Patrick will be conscious. Why don't we go get the tree? I think Patrick will want that tree."

"I agree."

Just then, a nurse walks out of the operating room and gives us the length of rope that I used to make the tourniquet. I take it from her and say, "We need that rope to tie the tree to the car."

"Are you the young lady who used it to make a tourniquet to save the boy's leg?"

Before I can answer, Dad says, "That's my daughter. She is going to be a nurse."

By the time Patrick gets home from the hospital, the tree is up and fully decorated. He is on crutches for most of the holiday, but every time he walks into the living room, he stops and admires his tree.

Life Lessons Learned:

My reaction to the accident with my brother, Patrick, showed me that I can maintain control under challenging conditions. That initial experience laid the foundation for me to be able to deal with patients in crisis for the rest of my life.

CHAPTER 30:

Our Relationship Changes

Through the winter, John and I become more comfortable with each other. I won't say we take each other for granted. We sometimes have, though, when our hormones push just a little too far. When those moments come, we back away from danger. I no longer am startled when he touches me. Nor does he flinch when I touch him. In the early stages, we explored each other whenever we could, within the boundaries we had set.

There are times John is holding me when I am thinking less about him and more about him going to college. He will leave me in Waterloo, Iowa, while he goes to Philadelphia. As we get closer to that separation moment, our passions cool down. We go to the prom, and have a great time, but our intimacy wanes.

We think about having a picnic by the lake like the previous summer, but we have yet to get around to it. I work more and more hours at the hospital. I am desperately trying to learn as much as possible. At the beginning of the summer, my wish comes true. After a year of working in many different departments within the hospital, I am called into my supervisor's office and told that my next assignment will be in the emergency room.

I can hardly hold in my excitement. I am finally going to be able to work in the place that I have always wanted to. Initially, I work behind the receptionist's desk, checking in people for care. This reception desk differs dramatically from the one I worked in during my first week at the hospital. I think I am prepared for the chaos and life and death pressure of an ER.

I go to my trusty library throughout the year to learn about the various departments I work in. I always study the operation of an ER more than anything else. I am told that when I report on Monday that I am to say hello to nurse Williams. She is the head nurse in the ER. She will give me instructions on what I am supposed to do.

School is over, and I have no final exams like last year. Before school is out, I make an appointment to speak with Sister Mary Martha, the school principal. The purpose is twofold.

First, I advise her that the nursing school needs a transcript of my grades at the end of my junior year. I am going to be applying on September 1st.

"It would mean a great deal to me if you wrote a recommendation letter."

"Of course," is her response, and then she asks, "Who else are you going to ask for letters of recommendation?"

"I am thinking about my biology teacher, pastor, and elementary school basketball coach."

"Why did you pick your basketball coach?"

"When I first entered the gym, he told me I was two years behind the other girls. If I wanted to play, I would have to work hard to catch up. In my last year, I was captain of the team. I hope the coach will tell the college about my determination and work ethic. I want the school to understand that I will work hard for the extraordinary opportunity that I will be given."

"Come by the school at the end of July, and I'll have your letter of recommendation ready for you along with your transcripts. Do they require you to write an essay?"

"Yes."

"I would be happy to help you with your essay, but I recommend you write about what you did to save your brother's leg."

Life Lessons Learned:

Relationships are only sometimes permanent. The passion of the moment may make us think that a relationship will last forever. I have learned that one of the many complex things we do is trust our heart to someone else.

CHAPTER 31:

The ER

I have waited one full year to get to work in the ER. Every day that I volunteer, I start my day by strolling through the ER. When my day is done, I exit the hospital by slowly walking through the ER. I listen to the discussion between the doctors, nurses, and patients. I begin to learn the language of the ER. In the beginning, I need help understanding many of the words. I write them down in my notebook. I go to the library to look them up to understand what is being said.

I hear a doctor say to the nurse to hang Ringer's lactate solution with a drip rate of 500 CC an hour. I had no clue what he was telling the first time I heard that command. In 24 hours, I know what it is and what it does for the patient. I always wave to the doctors, nurses, and orderlies. I learn their names so that when I get the opportunity to work there, I can call them by name.

On the first Monday in July, I walk into the ER scared to death. I see the head nurse, Pam Smith, for my instructions.

"Welcome, Miss Murphy, to our ER. Here is the first and most important rule while you are here: stay out of the way. I see you go through the ER every day. I can tell you are observing what is going on. However, watching from the outside differs from being in the middle of the action. Over time, if you are effective, you will get more responsibility. I'm the sole judge of your progress. I am the only person to make the decision if you can handle more responsibility.

"Most of the work you will be doing will be out of sight. Until I tell you differently, you will work at the reception desk checking in patients. Keep one thing in mind. When you are at the reception desk, you will be the first person from the hospital the patient sees. You have one job. You get the answers on the admission form. The more complete the records are, the better the medical history for the doctors is to figure out how to best help the patient."

Nurse Smith takes me to the reception desk and gives me an admission application, a clipboard, and a pen. She shows me where to get more copies of the form. She has one more command: "We can't treat people if we can't read their admission form. Write so that people can read it immediately. We don't have time to find you before we begin treatment. Losing precious time could be the difference between life and death."

This last statement shakes me. I don't expect to hear that. If I make a mistake, I may cause a patient to die.

"The tempo of the ER can change in a heartbeat. Things can be routine one moment and out of control the next. You will be an asset to the department if, when the panic comes, you can perform under fire. You need to begin to expect the unexpected."

We walk to the admissions desk. Nurse Smith introduces me to the three other people behind the desk. In front of each person are large letters of the alphabet. People are told to go to the letter corresponding to their last name's first letter. When things get hectic, all four of us behind the desk work to process the incoming patients, regardless of title. I am told that each day I will be behind a different letter.

Nurse Smith turns me over to one of the people behind the desk. She goes back to her office. She told me to stop by and see her when my shift was over.

About an hour into my shift, a man named Seth Adams comes up to me. I ask if he is here for help. He winces with pain, and he can hardly speak to say yes. I continued collecting more information until Adams says he is getting worse.

One of the other admission people says, "He needs a nurse right away."

I see him bending over. "Wait right here. I'm going to get a nurse."

I quickly scan the floor for a nurse, and I find one. I quickly run over to the nurse and explain the problem. The two of us return to the admission desk to see Mr. Adams. He is bent over in pain.

I bend over to try and help him up while the nurse rushes to get a wheelchair. In short order, they bring him a wheelchair. Just as the nurse is ready to wheel him to an examining room, an eruption comes out of his mouth. The contents of his stomach empty all over the front of her uniform. I look down, and I am covered with partially digested food and significant blood, too.

I can see the expression on Seth's face. He is sorry for what happened. I watch him being wheeled down the hallway. I pay little attention to the front of my uniform. The head nurse saw what had happened and says, "It comes with the job. You didn't panic. You stayed focused on the patient. Good job on your first day. Do you have a clean uniform to change into to finish your shift?"

"Yes, ma'am."

I agree I need to get out of these clothes. They are already beginning to smell. Nurse Smith takes me to the women's locker room. I get out of my dirty clothes, and as I stand in the shower, I let the warm water cascade down my body and watch all the debris wash down the drain.

I say to myself, "It is a great first day."

I get dressed and go back to work.

Life Lessons Learned:

I had waited for a long time to get this assignment. When the time came, I had doubts that I could handle it. I read many books on emergency room procedures, but reading books differs from actually being there.

Life is nothing more than a collection of experiences. It's like a big photo album you're given when you go out alone. Your album is full of blank pages. There must be a way of telling what pictures will be in your book. The first picture is the one we remember the most.

CHAPTER 32:

The Conversation

The summer passes quickly. At the end of July, I contact the four people I need for letters of recommendation. The only one who had a question is my basketball coach, Mr. Brown.

He calls the house and asks, "Why did you pick me? I have never written a letter of recommendation for a non-athlete college student."

"Coach, I picked you because you gave me an opportunity. You asked me to commit and said I showed you I could succeed."

"That you did."

"So, Coach, in your letter, just talk about the importance of committing and following through."

"No problem. I will give it to you next week. If you don't like what I say, let me know, and I'll change it."

John and I spend some time together in July. We hold each other, talking about what will happen to our relationship. It probably would be straightforward of me to give in to having sex with John before he goes to college. As much as I want him, I decide I can't take the chance. I don't want to get pregnant while he is off in Philadelphia. My first love is leaving me on August 15th. We have two weeks, and each time we are together, we get closer and closer.

On one of our last night's together, he unbuttons my blouse and puts his hand inside. He gently caresses my breast. I don't want him to let go. I think that this is the longest night of my life. We hold each other and make promises we fully intend to keep, but most never materialize. We will write to each other every week. We will see each other at Thanksgiving and Christmas. He promises to go with me to the senior prom, and then we will have time together during the summer.

I remind him that if I get into nursing school, most likely, the only time I can see him is the two weeks off I have in August. Lots of promises are made. We decide we are meant for each other if we can keep the relationship alive via long distance.

The following two weeks fly by. I ask to work more to take my mind off our pending separation. I am amazed that I have been working in the ER for two months. It is the most exhilarating thing I ever did in my life.

I live for the moment in the ER. I never know what is coming in those doors in the emergency room. Every day, I come home both exhilarated and at the same time exhausted. I am only working a three-hour shift. The doctors and nurses are working 12-hour shifts. I am in good shape. I can't imagine working a 12-hour shift five to six days a week.

I see everything — people with broken bones, gunshot wounds, stabbings. You name it, I saw it during those first two months. The most exciting thing I see, and still excites me today, is watching a baby being born. The rush of excitement is fantastic. Doctors and nurses who have done this hundreds of times are still excited when a baby is born. When I go home each day, I spend my time on the bus writing down questions and making observations about what I saw. I am starting my nurse training a year early.

When I wake, I look at the calendar in the kitchen where I had put a mark on August 15th. A simple heart is around John's name. He is going to be leaving at midday. He will stop by and see me on his way out of town. I hear the car pulling into our driveway. A door open and shuts, and he is coming up the front steps. The doorbell rings. I am the only one at home, so I answer it. I invite John in for just a few minutes before he must leave.

We hold each other for a long time. We only say something for a short time. We separate when John says, "I have to go. I'm going to miss holding you."

"I will miss you holding me."

We walk over to the front door. He takes me in his arms in the doorway behind the screen door and gives me a gentle, tender kiss. We separate and say goodbye. I tell him, "Please drive safely. Can you call me when you get to your dorm?"

He doesn't say anything. He steps on the porch and goes down the steps. When he reaches the bottom stage, he turns, looks up at me, and says, "Yes."

He gets into his car, pulls out of the driveway, and I wave and watch him drive down Myrtle Ave. into his new adventure. I walk back into the house, go upstairs to my bedroom, lay on my bed, and cry.

Life Lessons Learned:

Our lives are full of events – some good, some bad, some happy, and some sad. How we react to those events helps define who we are as a person. I will never forget my first love. My heart ached for a long time. I realized that our lives are like a book; every page is a part of who we are. If we are to grow and progress, we must turn the page.

CHAPTER 33:

Things Are Getting Worse

John is off to school in Philadelphia. The summer of 1930 is scorching, and the pond at the end of Myrtle Ave. is almost dry. In my travels to and from the hospital, I hear stories from the nurses and doctors about how bad the economy is. There are stories about banks beginning to fail. I listen to people's conversations, asking, "Do you have any money in Farmers Bank?"

The early winter of 1930 is a tough time in America. In December alone, 352 banks fail. Most of those are in the Midwest farm country.

One evening, when I get home from the hospital, my mother has a dinner plate on the stove for me. As I am finishing my dinner, my father comes into the kitchen.

"Dad, may I ask you a question?"

"Anytime. What is on your mind?"

"I hear much talk in the hospital that things are really getting difficult in the country. Banks seem to be failing, many people are losing their jobs, and things look scary. Are we going to be alright?"

My father comes over to the table. He pulls out the chair and sits next to me. "Are you concerned that we may not have the money to pay for your schooling?"

My father is a brilliant man. He has the wonderful gift of being able to read people. He can look into their souls to see what is bothering them.

"Mary Ellen, things are difficult in our country. The drought we are experiencing here in the Midwest is causing crops to fail. Farmers can't make the payments on their mortgages. The banks can foreclose on them, but they can't sell the farms to anybody because no one has the money to buy them. We have some money, though not very much, in our local bank. We have the bulk of our money invested in U.S. government bonds. The interest we earn on those bonds is more than enough to take care of the family and pay for your college. The machine shop is bustling. Your mother is making more practical and affordable dresses. She tells me that she is as busy as ever."

"May I ask you one more question?"

"Yes?"

"Do you think it will get much worse?"

"I don't think anybody knows for sure. I know that I don't know the answer. Many parts of our economy have been living in excess for some time. That speculation will have to be corrected. Now, Mary Ellen, may I ask you a question?"

"Of course," I say.

"Are we going to carry out the family tradition with you and Patrick and me finding the perfect Christmas tree?"

"Do you think that Patrick will be up to going out and chopping down a tree after last year?"

"You're right, probably not."

"So, how about you and I pick out the tree?"

"I would like that very much."

My mother and father continue to go to work every day. We are safe and secure. We have food on the table. My parents help other family members and neighbors whenever they can. My father is right about the Depression. It gets deeper. More banks fail, and more people become unemployed. We don't know long the Depression will last.

John doesn't make it home for Thanksgiving, but he makes it home for Christmas. He gets here from Philadelphia on the 22nd of December. The phone rings in the hallway. I race to pick it up. It is John.

"Can I come see you?" he says.

"Of course. I can't wait to see you."

"I'll be there in about 10 minutes."

I hear his car pull into the driveway. The sound of his tires on the gravel lifts my spirits from my talk with my father. I run out the front door and down the steps. Just as he is coming out of the car, I put my arms around him and kiss him.

"I can't tell you how much I've missed you and having you hold me," I say.

"I feel the same way."

"Would you like to go get something to eat?"

"Can we go to the drive-thru and get food to go? I want some quiet place where we can be together."

"I'd like that very much. Let's go."

We get in the car. Before we pull out of the driveway, we turn to each other. I reach over and take his hand. While we are kissing, I move his hand to my breast. Our mouths part, and I say, "John, I've missed that."

"I've missed it, too. We should do more of it before I leave."

"Absolutely."

We spend as much time together as possible. Christmas comes and goes, and John must go back to school. With all the sadness in the world, I need some joy.

Life Lessons Learned:

Adversity can be all around us, yet not directly impact us. We may be fine, while many people are not. We must empathize with those struggling and share some of the gifts God has given us to help others the best we can.

CHAPTER 34:

Now It's Time to Wait

I pick up everything I need to complete my application for nursing school — the letters of recommendation, the transcript of my grades, and the essay that Sister Mary Martha helped me write. I complete the application and take it to Miss Martin to review and ensure everything is correct. I ask all the letter writers to give me two copies. I make a copy of the essay and the application. I put the duplicate copies in a large brown envelope and put it in my dresser drawer. I get another envelope and address it to the Dean of Admissions. After school, I put everything in and seal the envelope.

The next day, I stop at the post office to mail my future. Once I give it to the postal clerk, I can only wait. I am submitting my application just as I begin my senior year, and I know from our discussion at the school visit to expect a decision by January 1st. There is nothing else I can do. There is no point in getting nervous, because I can only wait and pray.

This day is emotional for me for several reasons. The application and its outcome are totally out of my control. I am excited about it being done. I am also somewhat depressed that maybe I won't get in. I have no backup plan. Then, it dawns on me. I should look at the local nursing school as a backup. I decided to collect all the documents again. I will stop by the local nursing school to get an application. I am excited about having a backup plan, and the idea that I do have a plan lifts my spirits.

When I get to the ER, I say hello to everybody. Now, things are quiet. I put my things away and walk into the lobby to my workstation. I can see the ambulance pulling into the portico. Two doctors and nurses rush outside as they bring the person out of the ambulance on a gurney. The doctors and nurses do a quick evaluation. I hear the doctor say that the man is in cardiac arrest.

I stand still as they wheel the gurney past me. I realize he is a relatively young man. I would guess he is in his 40s. They are taking him to trauma room one. I am working on restocking all the supply cabinets in the trauma rooms that day. The man on the stretcher is in trauma room one. I see the team of doctors and nurses working frantically to save him.

I am across the hall, stocking trauma room two. I can see what is going on in the room across the hallway. The team is trying everything they can to keep this man alive. It is orchestrated chaos. I finally hear the lead doctor say, "Time of death, 4:47 p.m."

The machines are turned off, one by one. The team begins to leave the trauma room. The room empties quickly. I stand there. For the first time in my life, I watched somebody die. For a while, I couldn't move. For some reason, I am drawn to the room where the body lies. I start to walk towards him, not knowing why. When I get to the foot of the bed, I stand there. I look at him. I can sense tears welling up in my eyes for somebody I don't know. He is a total stranger to me. After a moment, I silently say a prayer for the man's soul.

Behind me, one of the ER nurses comes in and quietly asks, "What are you doing?"

I turn and tell her, "This is the first person I've ever seen die. I am praying for him. What happens next?"

"We get him ready to go to the morgue. The mortuary will come and pick him up and prepare him for burial. While we're preparing the body, this room needs to be cleaned."

I ask her, "What can I do?"

"Well, you can't help with the body. You can clean up all the debris on the floor and put it in bags for disposal."

Two people come into the room to help clean up. I say to the person in charge of cleaning the room, "I would like to help."

When both teams are finished, a clean white sheet is draped over the body. A waiting morgue attendant comes to collect it.

Life Lessons Learned:

I would continually replay that scene in my brain for the longest time afterward. Eventually, it diminished but never fully went away. To this day, so many years later, I still remember that experience.

Over the 20 years since that man passed away, I have experienced many soldiers and civilians who died under my care. It has never been easy, but if you are going to succeed, you must learn to deal with death and disappointment, because if you can't, you can't be an ER nurse.

CHAPTER 35:

The Answer

My senior year of high school is uneventful. I continue to do my work and my studies. I get excellent grades in both. The hospital agrees to send a letter of recommendation to both colleges about my career as a volunteer. Christmas comes, but it is different this year. If I hear from the college, it might be my last Christmas at home for several years. John returns on the 21st, and we spend as much time together as possible. He clearly is still interested in me. When he leaves to go back to Philadelphia, I never feel more alone.

Each day in January, I run home to see if there is any mail. I am looking for a letter from the college, but I am still waiting for something to come. I have filled out my application and sent it to the local nursing school, and I am still waiting to hear from them too. I feel like nobody wants me. If that is the case, what will I do after high school?

The economy is getting worse and worse. Businesses and shops are closing. For-sale signs on houses and farms are an indication that things are horrible all over town. My family tries to help our extended family. We give food to our neighbors and small amounts of money. Those who have work are saying it might get even worse.

I am so proud of my parents. They are trying to help as many people as possible. They may not be the wealthiest people in the world, but they are certainly some of the most generous. When Spring comes, my father increases the size of our garden. There is more than enough for us so that he can share with the neighbors. I see neighbors following my father's lead. They increase the size of their gardens so that they can share with those in need. My mother cans fruits and vegetables to tide us over the winter. My dad continues to raise chickens. Each morning he collects the eggs, and each week he prepares a hen for Sunday dinner.

I come home from the hospital on January 15th. Mother meets me at the door and says, "You have two envelopes."

I ask, "Where are they?"

"By the telephone."

I run down the hallway and see the two envelopes. The first thing I do is look at the return addresses on both. One is from Chicago. One is from Waterloo. I wonder to myself which one I should open first. I decide on Waterloo. I tear open the envelope. I take out the letter. It says that I have been accepted at the school of nursing.

I am thrilled because I know I have something to do after high school. Then, I turn and pick up the second envelope. I open it and slowly read the letter inside:

"Dear Miss Murphy, this letter is to inform you that you have been selected for the incoming class at St. James School of Nursing in Chicago, Illinois. We are excited about having you join us. We'll be sending you more information throughout the next few months.

"There is one condition governing this letter of acceptance. We do not believe there will be any problems for you, but it is a college rule. Upon completing your senior year, you must submit to us within two weeks the transcript of your final year grades. Any significant decline in your grade point average could cause us to rescind this acceptance letter.

"We look forward to seeing you in late August. Should you have any ques-tions, please feel free to call or write."

The letter was signed by Sister Mary Francis, the Dean of Admissions.

My parents are standing at the door to the kitchen, looking down the hallway. They can see me where I am standing.

I turn to them, run down the hall, put my arms around both, and say, "Both schools have accepted me!"

My parents express their pride. My father asks, "Which one do you choose?" He asks that with a big smile on his face.

My mother adds, "It looks like we're going to make trips to Chicago."

I ask my parents if I can call John and tell him.

My father says, "Yes, you've earned it. Share it with your friend."

I let go of my parents. My brother and older sister are not home, so I go upstairs to my room, sit on the edge of my bed, and reread both letters. My thoughts turn to the unknowns on this journey. I commit that I will become the best possible nurse I can be.

Life Lessons Learned:

I became the first member of our family from both sides to attend college. My parents' belief in me gave me the fortitude to set a goal. I made them a promise to do my best to achieve it. Sometimes, we set goals to see the results immediately. Yet other times, the results of all the hard work to achieve that goal take considerable time.

I learned things from my parents that I carry with me today. I tell all the nurses I've been training over my career to never give up on people. Try to be the very best that you can be.

CHAPTER 36:

Prom

The last half of my senior year comes very rapidly. We have the junior-senior prom in May, and John, as promised, comes back to be my escort. Then, there is my graduation and my valedictory speech. I am done with our Lady of Victory High School.

John is just in for a few days. He must go back to get ready for finals. We go to the prom and stay for a while, then leave. I want to get something to eat and talk about John and me.

I look forward to spending time with John when he comes home for summer break. I must make sure he understands that I will be leaving to go to Chicago, probably in mid-August. The next time I see him will be a year from now, because I only have two weeks off. I can't come home until then because of my schedule.

He seems surprised when I speak to him about what will happen. I remind him that we did talk about this some time ago, and he needs to remember.

"When I have breaks, could I stop and see you in Chicago?"

My heartbeat quickens when he indicates that he wants to work around the schedule so we can see each other. "I don't know the restrictions about visitors or how much time off I will have. As soon as I get there, I'll find out what the rules are, and I'll let you know."

Saturday evening is the prom. A part of me doesn't want to go, but I want to be with John. I don't ask my mother to make me a new dress. I wore the one from last year. I have not tried it on before the big night. I am a different person this year. I have more deep curves. My chest is fuller and rounder, and so are my hips. My waist is smaller. The dress fits my body like a glove when I try it on. Because it fits so snugly, it emphasizes all my curves.

I call my mother to come and look at me in the dress. When she sees me, I can see the look of amazement on her face. She says, "My little girl is no longer little or a girl. You're a beautiful woman. You should get a lot of attention at the prom."

John comes to pick me up, and when he sees me, he says, "You are the most beautiful woman I have ever seen."

We get in the car to drive to the prom. He reaches over to kiss me, puts his hand on my breast, and whispers in my ear, "I have a condom in my pocket. I'm prepared."

I whisper, "For now, just keep it in your pocket."

"Why don't we go and let me show you off to everyone? They need to see you in that dress."

He takes me around the dance floor, showing off his prize. I enjoy being the center of attention but feel like a show pony after a while and want to leave. We go to dinner by ourselves. Then, we get in the car and find a place to park. I don't know where. We spend a couple of hours all over each other. I have no inhibitions with John. I let him do almost whatever he wants to do. He is always gentle and considerate. He never pushes, but he has the softest hands, which are warm. When we have had enough intimacy, we button up our clothes and sit close together.

I turn to John, "You've almost finished your first year of college. This is very hard for me to ask. Have you met anybody that you're interested in spending time with?"

He doesn't answer.

"I know that in our relationship, we never went all the way. We never had sex. I'm sure that was frustrating for you." I don't want to ask the question, but I need to find out. "Have you found somebody to make love to?"

The expression on John's face shows he is startled. He doesn't say anything for a while, then he speaks.

"I've spent time with many people at school, mostly guys. I have met a couple of girls. I think something could develop with one of them, but I'm not sure. I have not had sex with her, though. She's not quite as attractive as you, but she is very desirable. I don't know where it's going or if it's going anywhere."

I tell him, "John, you've been a great friend. We have both learned about each other and our passions. Thank you for all the intimate experiences you gave me. We had a lot of good times and a lot of fun. I'll remember them for the rest of my life. What's the young lady's name?"

"Helen Wilson."

"Where is she from?"

"Pittsburgh."

"Is she an engineering student?"

"Yes, and very smart like you. Perhaps even smarter than me."

I turn to him, face-to-face, and put both of my hands on his cheeks. I say to him in a very low voice, "I'm happy for you. I hope she turns out to be the one."

We sit back in our seats and don't say anything for the longest time.

Then, he turns to me and says, "You will always have a special place in my heart. I promise to tell you what happens between Helen and me."

John starts the car, takes me home, and before I leave, he kisses me good night. We agree to have breakfast the following day at the diner before he heads off to Philadelphia. It is not meant to be.

Life Lessons Learned:

First loves are important, because they help establish our value system. We learn to understand what other people are thinking. Do they have respect and compassion for us? Or, are they only out for themselves and what they can get from us?

Love is a powerful emotion. Often, it causes us to make more mistakes than anything else. Real love is finding a partner you want and hope to spend the rest of your life with. This is often different from a first love. The physical attraction between a man and a woman is powerful. Sometimes – no, most of the time – raging hormones are the worst thing you can have in trying to make a life decision.

CHAPTER 37:

The Valedictorian

By the middle of my senior year, I suspect that I will be asked to be the valedictorian at the graduation ceremony. By the end of March, Sister Mary Martha sends me a note asking me to meet with her at the end of the school day. I knock on the door and hear Sister say, "Come in."

I sit down in the chair in front of her desk. Sister Mary Martha is always kind to me. She was encouraging when I told her I wanted to attend nursing school.

"Not that you will be surprised, but the faculty has decided that you should be given the honor of the valedictory address for graduation."

I tell Sister, "I had anticipated the possibility. Now that it is here, I am somewhat overwhelmed and honored to be asked."

Sister Mary Martha suggests that I think about what I want to say. Then, I am to come back to her. We will sit down and discuss what I will say and if it is acceptable to her and the faculty.

"It should be something you believe in that you want to say."

I tell her that I will think about it and come back in a couple of weeks and share my thoughts with her.

I leave the school to go to the hospital. As I look out the bus's window, I see many for-sale signs on houses and businesses that are boarded up because they have no business or not enough business. More banks have failed. Waterloo, Iowa, and the rest of the United States are in the throes of the Great Depression. I have the opportunity each day when I leave the hospital to pick up the newspaper and read what is happening in our country. I am probably more aware of the impact of the Depression than many of my classmates.

It is difficult to tell if some of my classmates' parents have lost their jobs, but I know some are on the verge of losing their homes. Sometimes reading the stories about homeless people and soup kitchens is hard. I read about people with no money, no hope, and no prospects. When I read all the stories about the economy and our opportunities, would my school still be able to take me in just about six months?

I fully expect, any day, that I will get a letter from St. James School of Nursing that they are closing their doors, and there would not be an opportunity for me.

When I come home from the hospital in mid-April, 1931, my mother says there is a letter for me by the telephone.

I ask her, "Who is it from?"

She responds, "The School of Nursing in Chicago."

I am worried that it is going to be bad news. I walk down the hallway and see the letter leaning against the telephone. I pick it up, open it, and start to read it. It is from the Dean of Students. She says that they are looking forward to seeing me in mid-August. She reminds me that I need to send her my grades for the entire senior year. As previously stated in other correspondence, she notes that my admission is contingent on me having maintained my GPA.

I start to cry. My mother runs down the hallway, asking, "Is its bad news?"

With giant tears running down my cheeks, I turn to my mother and give her the letter. She reads it, and she begins to cry. We hug each other, and she says, "You are going to be a spectacular nurse."

My father comes home, entering through the back door. He can hear my mother and me crying. He rushes down the hallway, asking, "What's going on? Why are you crying?"

My mother says, "We're crying because our daughter will go to nursing school, even in a terrible depression."

My father puts his arms around both my mother and me, giving us a hug only a father can give. He says, "I was never in doubt."

A few tears run down his cheeks, too.

For some reason, I need to leave the house. I tell my mother I want to go out for a short walk and that I will be back to eat my dinner. I can't remember the last time I have been at the park at the end of Myrtle Ave. Then, it dawns on me that it was the picnic with John. For some reason, I want to go back to the park.

As I walk toward the park, though, something is different. What I see in front of me, I don't expect. What I was seeing scared me.

Perhaps about a dozen small fires are burning in the park. As I get closer, I see several tents. Some are large, but I also see some shanties. I realize that homeless people are living in the same park in which, not that long ago, I almost lost my virginity to John.

My determination to succeed as a nurse stopped events that could've put me in one of the shanties. I don't go into the park, and I don't think anybody sees me. I turn around and go back to my house.

I tell my parents what I saw.

"Is there anything we can do for those people?" I ask.

My father says, "Tomorrow is Saturday. Why don't we, as a family, go to the park? Let's meet the people and see if there's anything we can do to help them?"

We all agree with Dad.

Life Lessons Learned:

Sometimes it's essential to stop and look at the people before you. Are they hurting physically or mentally? Before you can help them, you must assess their needs. If you take the time to figure out the problem before you solve it, you will be more successful.

In the Depression, people needed work – not a soup kitchen. Spend a little extra time getting to know a person before you offer a solution.

CHAPTER 38:

A Visit to the Park and Graduation

We wake up the following day to the oven's most wonderful aroma of bread baking.

Another smell differs from what I'd normally think of at breakfast time. Whatever it is, it is enticing. I get dressed and go downstairs into the kitchen.

On the table are two dozen long loaves of homemade bread. On the stove is a massive pot of beef and vegetable soup, and on the strainer by the sink is two dozen Mason jars with lids and rings.

"What are you doing?" I ask my mother.

"We are going to take this bread and this soup to the people at the end of Myrtle Avenue. I want to make sure they have something to eat. Your father and I have decided that each Saturday, as long as we can do it, we will take 12 loaves of bread and 12 jars of soup to the people in the park."

At that moment, I know what I will say to my classmates on graduation day:

> We are about to leave the school which has been our home for the last four years. Many of our fellow citizens are homeless and hungry. As we move out into the world and take on the responsibilities of the next

generation, we must stop and make sure we share what we have with people with low incomes and the homeless. Some of us will be going off to college in faraway places. Even in those cities, there will be people who can use our help.

Think about forming groups that could help at soup kitchens and shelters. Gain your education in the classroom but learn from the people you serve. As Jesus tells us, love our neighbor as ourselves. We must share the blessings the Lord gives us. No matter how small the gift, we must give to the less fortunate.

I do not doubt that America will recover from this Great Depression. When it does, prosperity will be there for all of us. We must learn from our mistakes to avoid making them again. No matter how prosperous we become as a nation, Jesus told us the poor will be with us forever. As you move onto the next chapter of your life, never forget what you learned here at this school, the friends you have made, the teachers you love, and the families that supported you in earning this education. As you become successful, you must ask yourself regularly, "What am I doing to care for God's children?"

We go to the park and distribute our bread and soup. The people are very appreciative. My family knows we are doing what the Lord told us to do. When I get home, I go up to my room and put my thoughts for my valedictory address on paper. When I am done, I put them in my book bag and go downstairs to be with my family.

Monday morning, I stop by the principal's office and drop off my notes of what I want to say to my classmates for Sister to review. I stop by the principal's office to see Sister Mary Martha. I knock on the door.

Sister Mary Martha gets up and comes around her desk. She touches my shoulder and says, "Your words are beautiful. I wouldn't change a thing. That's your speech."

I thank Sister, and I give my address just as I wrote it. The address is a little short. I had not shared it with my parents. They hear it for the first time at the graduation ceremony. Afterward, they come up to me and tell me how wonderful it is and how proud they are of what I've said and who I am. My father splurges and takes us out to dinner to celebrate my graduation.

Life Lessons Learned:

Sometimes in life, we are allowed to make an impression on people. My job at my graduation speech was to tell my classmates what our responsibilities could be when we left the school. The opportunities would be there if we look for them. If we see them, the question remains, can we capture the moment?

No matter how hard they look, some people can't tell when someone else is hurting. Broken bones and cuts are all visible signs that somebody is breaking and are easy to detect. More difficult to ascertain is when a person has a broken heart.

CHAPTER 39:

I'm Going to be a Nurse

John is home for summer vacation. We spend a lot of our free time together. Every time we are together, there is intimacy. Eventually, we're just sitting in the car, staring out the windshield. Both of us are very reluctant to raise the subject of what will happen to us.

We talk about him stopping by as he travels back and forth from Philadelphia. We could get together when I am home for my short vacation. Do we want to get together? Just about a week before I am ready to head to Chicago to start my journey to become a nurse, we finally talk about ourselves.

I start the conversation.

"John, I have grown so much as a person and a woman being with you. I can't thank you enough for all that you shared with me. I know it must've been highly frustrating for you that our intimacy was never consummated. I know it was for me. I would love it if you could visit me on your way to and from Philadelphia. I understand if you don't. Based on listening to you about how much you love Philadelphia, it's not likely that you'll come back to Waterloo to live and work. In many respects, you are like me. Waterloo might be a great place to grow up, but it's not a place I want to live long term. We both must get out. In so doing, we are going our separate ways. I will miss you terribly. I hope you will miss me. I hope that we will always be friends."

John thinks for a moment, then responds:

"Mary Ellen, when I first saw you, I was like every other teenage boy in Waterloo who thought you looked magnificent. The one thing we all had in common was that we would give anything to see you naked. Do you know how jealous all those boys would be if they knew I had seen that magnificent body? We practiced our skill of being intimate with each other without sex. I honestly believe I would not have grown as a man if I'd just had sex with you. I don't know what happened to our relationship, but I know we must move on. The things that we explored, I hope, will make both of us better lovers when we find the right person to spend the rest of our life with.

"I can't tell you how much I will miss having that magnificent body and your tender soul to hold in my arms. I hope we will always be friends. When we see each other again, we shouldn't be afraid to intro-duce ourselves as best friends. I can't make a commitment that I'll write to you regularly. I'll try to send you something, and you can respond with something. I do want to hear what's happening in your life. I want to know how you're progressing as a human being and especially as a terrific nurse. I need to get home. I want to pick you up in the morning for breakfast. On the day you leave, I'll stop by to see you off. I'll give you a kiss goodbye and maybe just one more hug and a squeeze."

We have breakfast the following day. I have about a week before I am departing for Chicago. The hospital throws me a goodbye party. I cry when they cry, but I tell them I will stop by when I return. I go around the town saying goodbye to some of my friends. I pack my bags, and I am ready to go. I call John and say, "I am leaving in the morning at 8 o'clock. If you still want to say goodbye. I'd love to see you."

I can't sleep. I am excited about everything behind me and, at the same time, excited about what lies ahead of me. My dad loads the suit-cases in the car. John arrives and parks his car at the edge of the driveway. I go down to see him. He gets out of the car and stays on his side. The vehicle is between my parents and us. He takes me in his arms and kisses me. I get one last squeeze on the left side. We say goodbye, and he leaves.

My sister and brother come out. I kiss and hug them goodbye. We get in the car and head east to the next adventure in my life. As we drive through Waterloo and all the other towns on our way to Chicago, we can see the devastation of the Depression, houses for sale, and empty buildings. It is scorched. We've had no rain for a long time, so occasionally, there is a massive dust storm. We must roll up the car windows to keep the dirt from coming inside.

My check-in day is Sunday. We decide to stay at the same hotel as on our first visit. We arrive on Saturday night. They will take me to the nursing school the following day. After they say goodbye, they will head back to Waterloo.

We get to the hotel at about 7 p.m. on Saturday. Like before, we have adjoining rooms. I leave the connecting door open for the longest time. My mother finally comes and closes the door so the others can get some sleep. When she does that, I am alone in the room and, quite honestly, scared. I have read as much as possible about the school, the curriculum, the people, and the teachers. I will meet 49 girls my age, or thereabouts, who are some of the best and brightest in the country. They come here to this prestigious nursing school to be the country's best nurses.

I don't know what time I finally fall asleep. We must be at the school at 9 o'clock. I set my alarm for seven. When it rings, it startles me.

I realize where I am. I quickly get up, shower, dress, and I am ready for breakfast. We finish eating at about 8:15. We go to the room to collect our bags. I come down, and the car is waiting for us.

The doorman asks my father, "Do you know where you're going?"

"Yes, sir, we're taking my daughter to the nursing school."

He tells my father, "Congratulations, I hope she makes a great nurse."

He responds, "She will be one of the best."

Life Lessons Learned:

One of the scariest things we must do in life is move away from home for the first time. We leave from one place and go to another. Where we come from is home, family, and friends. Where I am headed is to be with total strangers. I hope they will become family and friends.

To strike out on your own to go to a new town or city and start a new life is hard. Only a few people will do that. During the time of the Great Depression, people would not take the risk of leaving their homes and hearts. Many families are forced to strike out and do something new. I've always been the kind of person to want change. That's why I left Waterloo. I had to see something of the world. The only way to do that was to leave Waterloo. As this story unfolds, you will see me going through the next stage of my life.

CHAPTER 40:

I'm on My Own

I leave my two suitcases at the curb. I say goodbye to my parents. We hug and kiss and cry. They must leave, and I must get on with the rest of my life. I watch as they leave, and I wave until they are gone. I turn around and look up at the building. A big banner on the front of the building says, "Welcome to the Class of 1934."

I go up to the front door. Sister Mary Frances meets me in the foyer.

"Welcome to St. James, Miss Mary Ellen Murphy. Please follow me to the registration desk. You'll get your room assignment, and somebody will help you get your bags to your room. Lunch will be served in the cafeteria at noon with an orientation at 1 p.m."

I go to the registration desk. I get my room key and am told I will be in room 212. The Sister registering me says, "Go up the stairs and then turn to the left at the first landing. Go down the hallway. Your room will be on the right-hand side."

She asks if I need help with the suitcase. I reply, "I could use help with one."

She introduces me to Mr. Mahoney, who will help me with my bags. He picks up my bags, and the door to my room opens when we arrive. I ask him to put the bags on the bed and thank him for his help.

I wait to unpack. I sit on my bed, looking at the room bigger than the room I shared with my sister. It is all mine. I walk out in the hallway and go to the bathroom. It has six showers with partitions. I see six toilets with partitions but no bathtubs. I go back to my room and look at my watch. I have about 30 minutes to get unpacked. I must be in the cafeteria but can't remember where it is. I need help. I step out into the hallway, and most doors are closed. I assume that the other students have already moved in ahead of me. I go across the hallway to room 211 and knock on the door.

The door opens, and a dark-haired, olive-skinned, beautiful woman appears. She says, "You're gorgeous. What's your name?"

"My name is Mary Ellen Murphy, and I'm in 212."

She says her name is Marie Bella. "Where are you from, Red?"

I am shocked that she calls me Red. I let it pass. In fact, from that moment on, people called me Red for the rest of my life.

She continues, "With a name like Mary Ellen Murphy, you must be Irish."

"With a name like Marie Bella, you must be Italian. Where are you from?"

"New York City. Brooklyn, actually."

"Are you unpacked?"

"Yes, are you?"

"Yes."

"Let's go have lunch."

The two of us walk down the hall. Other girls start to come out of their dorm rooms. We all head toward the stairway to go downstairs for lunch. Rather than ask where the cafeteria was, I'll follow everybody else. Why not let somebody else ask for directions? I will follow the crowd.

When we get to the cafeteria, not only are the 50 first-year students waiting, but also there are students from years two and three all having lunch simultaneously. The setup is much like the cafeteria at my high school — serving lines with trays. Plates and silverware are stacked up. We slowly go down the line, hold our plates, and tell the server what we want. There are a series of round tables where we sit together.

Marie and I go to a table, and before long, six other girls are sitting with us. We introduce ourselves to each other and talk about where they are from. There are young women from all over the country in the school. I don't share a lot with them because I just met them. Over time, these women will become my new sisters. I could almost share anything with them. They are the best and the brightest. I would understand just how smart they are as I got into classes with them.

I finish my food and listen to the conversation. We take our trays to the cleaning area when lunch is over. I have about 40 minutes before the 1 o'clock orientation. Again, I am still determining where the direction is going to be.

We leave our rooms and go down the hallway to the stairs. Like before, I follow the students to the auditorium, where the orientation will begin. I do not know that orientation will take three days. We learn all the rules about campus life, proper behavior when classes start, where the infirmary is, and how to get to the hospital. At the end of my first day, my head is spinning. How am I ever going to remember all this stuff? Exhausted, I walk out of the auditorium with Marie.

I say to her, "Did you get all of that?"

"No, I figured you would."

With that, we both laugh. "We've got a lot to catch up on if we are going to make it through the first week."

When I return to my room, I realize I have not opened the closet, because all my clothes fit in the dresser. I walk over to the closet and open the door. Hanging on wooden hangers are three nurse uniforms.

I have white stockings, shoes, and a plain nurse's hat. I stare at them for the longest time. What will it be like to wear them?

Marie and I go to dinner. We remember the way.

At dinner, Sister tells us, "Tomorrow, you wear your uniforms."

I am so excited I can't sleep. I set my alarm clock for half an hour earlier than I need to get up. I want to insure I am properly dressed before leaving for the day.

Life Lessons Learned:

Uniforms are a way to distinguish one profession from another; a soldier wears his uniform, and it's different than a mail carrier or doctor. If you see a woman in a white dress with a white cap, you assume she must be a nurse. If you know someone in a long white coat, you assume they are a doctor. I started every day for the rest of my life ensuring I had a clean and pressed uniform. I was proud to be a nurse and didn't mind showing off.

CHAPTER 41:

So Much to Learn

Over the next three days, we discuss what will happen during the next three years in incredible detail. On the 4th day, we visit all the classrooms, labs, and the hospital. We receive a weekly schedule of our daily classes and are told about our hospital assignments. We accept the day and times we are to work in the hospital.

On Friday, we visit the bookstore to get the textbooks we need for the next three months of school. We receive paper, pen, and ink for daily notes. We are told to review class notes each evening. The schedule gives us the dates we will take tests and the final exams for the quarter.

Marie and I, along with the other women, walk back to the dorm with our arms full of books. I go into my room and drop all the stuff on my desk. I walk over to my bed and collapse. I am exhausted. Before I realize it, I am fast asleep. I hear knocking on my door. For a moment, I am back at the hotel when we came here for the first time. I think it is my mom knocking on my connecting door.

I get out of bed and go open my door. Standing there is Marie.

"Are you coming to dinner? You look like you have been asleep."

"Yes, I want dinner, and I have been asleep. Give me a minute to splash water on my face and brush my hair."

I am still groggy but perk up as we approach the cafeteria.

Marie and I move along the food line and fill our plates. Sister tells us, "You should eat with different people for the first few weeks of school. It also is a good idea to mix with other classes. This way you can meet many people from different parts of the country. You can learn about them and why they want to be a nurse."

We have the first weekend off. We are told that we will work during the next week and the following weekend in the hospital as scheduled.

I meet more of my classmates and second and third-year nurses. Mixing us up is a good idea so we can talk to more people. I meet a lot of attractive women from different backgrounds than mine. It is still fascinating to me to speak to other people. Dinner is over, and I am ready to return to my room and go to bed.

Maria and I talk about the people we had dinner with. I'm going to like her a lot. Her New York accent is funny. She has a good heart and good opinions on everything.

I say good night to Marie and go to my room. I put my towel and washcloth on my arm, go to the bathroom to wash my face, and get ready for bed.

Tomorrow will be a hectic day. I need rest to be at my best on the first day of school. I look at my schedule for the week and see my classes begin at 9 a.m. Lunch is from 12 to 12:30. I have afternoon classes till 5 o'clock. Dinner is at 6 o'clock, and on Mondays, Wednesdays, and Fridays, I report to the hospital at 7:30 p.m. I work in the hospital until 9:30. When I finish, I return to my room for some well-earned sleep.

I report to the hospital on Saturday at 9:30 a.m., and my shift is till 4:30. On Sundays, I work from noon to 7 p.m. As I look at my schedule for the next month, I will be off work at the hospital every other weekend. I can hardly read anymore. I put the schedule down, crawl into my bed, and immediately sleep.

I'm up early. This is the first day wearing my uniform, which I will be proud to wear for the rest of my life.

In short order, I adjust to the work and class schedule and do very well. I feel comfortable but stimulated — not only in the schoolwork, but also in the hospital work. We only have one phone for us to use for the whole floor. In the middle of September, I get a knock at the door. I am told that I have a phone call. I am afraid that something is wrong at home. I rush to the phone to see what the problem is.

To my surprise, it is John on the phone. He tells me he is leaving for Philadelphia the next day and wants to know if I can see him the following day. As luck would have it, I don't have a hospital assignment in the evening.

I learn in orientation that there are strict rules on the conduct of nursing students. Men are not permitted on the dorm floors. I can go out for an evening, but I must be back in my room by 10:30. I tell John I would love to see him.

I take a moment to explain the rules, and he says, "That is fine. We'll just go to dinner. I'll get you back long before 10:30."

I realize I have been a little homesick. It is great to hear his voice. I am excited about seeing him tomorrow. I ask him, "Do you have directions to the school?" He says that he does. "Then, I'll see you tomorrow. Good night, John."

Life Lessons Learned:

In high school, I ate lunch with the same girlfriends every day. What happened is that we had the same friends through high school. There were people in my graduating class I didn't even know.

When Sister suggested that we dine around to experience other people, I saw it as a chance to expand my relationships. I need exposure to people with different values, beliefs, and cultures.

In many hospitals, the nursing staff is more susceptible to turnover than any other medical professional. I suggest to all the nursing staff that there should be social interactions, because these interactions ultimately make us better nurses.

CHAPTER 42:

My First Crisis

I sit in my psychology class when my teacher discusses depression. She speaks of how the nation, because of the Great Depression, is experiencing an epidemic of mental illness. Sometimes, people become so depressed and lonely that they want to hurt themselves and commit suicide.

I have not had the opportunity to leave campus. I am curious to know what the neighborhood around the school is like. I have yet to go to downtown Chicago. I have two reference points: Waterloo, Iowa, and the towns and villages between Waterloo and Chicago.

I see people are unemployed, houses are for sale, and businesses are closed in Waterloo and the places in between. It must've been depressing for those families whose breadwinner had lost his job. Without a job and no income, they are evicted from their home. People are begging for food to try and survive. People are looking for handouts so they can make it through the day.

The teacher says, "We will see depression as nurses, specifically when working in a community hospital. As you progress through your schooling, you will see the face of the Great Depression."

I remember the people at the homeless camp at the end of my street. I recall seeing the faces when we took bread and soup to them. I could see the smiles on their face, but I also saw the sadness in their eyes. I am struck with sorrow as I think about the suffering all over this great country. I start to cry.

My classmates and the teacher see what is happening. They ask me if I am all right. I tell them, "The sadness is so strong that it overpowers me for the moment, and I don't know how to deal with it."

The instructor says, "It's not uncommon for people like you who have this great desire to help people to become overwhelmed by the sadness and the depression people are feeling today. We can and should talk about it, but we must also remember to care for our patients."

The teacher continues, "You should discuss your expectations in coming to St. James. Not everybody who comes to St. James will ultimately be a nurse. History has shown that roughly about 10% of the students who start on day one never make it to graduation. Some find out quickly, while others conclude that nursing is not for them. I admire all of you for wanting to become nurses, and any of you who decide that it's not for you are not diminished in any way in my thoughts of you. Nursing is an honorable profession. It is hard, and sometimes it's sad. But at times, it is full of joy, like when you see a baby born or have a patient come out of a coma when you've been sitting by their bedside for hours. I am here every day, and if you want to talk, please stop by.

"If I'm not in my office, you can make an appointment. One of the most challenging things in your job is not judging patients when treating them, regardless of their ailments. During a depression, your patient may not be clean. They may not have the best clothes or even be starving. As nurses, we take care of the body but must also be sensitive to the soul's needs. I would like to see a show of hands of how many of you in this room have homeless people in your hometown, vacant buildings, and families that have lost their homes."

I look around, and every hand goes up.

She continues, "I want you to look around and see how many hands are in the air. You are from all over the country. The number of hands in the air should indicate how much desperation and depression is in our country today. If you can show kindness to one patient who's homeless or out of work, you will give them hope that somebody does care for them. We have a textbook you must study in this class for future reference. I am required to teach from that textbook. We will also learn about psychology by sharing our real-life experiences daily."

My tears stop. I feel better for two reasons. One reason is that the class will help me deal with what is happening in our country. The second reason is that, in a short while, John is coming to see me.

Life Lessons Learned:

Sometimes, medical professionals are criticized for their poor bedside manner, while others have spectacular ones. In my career of supervising nurses, one of the things I must work on is improving their bedside manner. They must show compassion and empathy for all their patients, regardless of personal biases. Contrary to the proverb, making a silk purse from a sow's ear is possible. You must work at it.

CHAPTER 43:

I'm Different with John

I regain my composure after breaking down in psychology class. Marie catches up as I work my way back to the dorm and asks, "Are you okay?"

I respond, "I am fine. This is the first time I've been away from my family. I have been dealing with homesickness, but I feel better that I got it out today. I'm not sure I'm genuinely looking forward to seeing John this evening. It will be nice to see somebody from home, although part of me is unsure."

Marie and I walk to our room. I sit on the edge of my bed with Marie sitting beside me. "From what you told me, John is special to you."

"He is, but he's moving on just like I am. He represents a beautiful thing from my past. Unless I'm wrong, I don't see any future with John. We will always be special friends but never lovers or husband and wife."

"What time is he coming?"

"I'm going to meet him downstairs at 7:30. I've got time to pull myself together to get ready to see him."

"Well, Red, I hope things go well for you tonight. Knock on my door when you get back."

Marie leaves and goes to her room. I sit on the bed a little longer, and when I look at the clock, it is almost 7. I go to my closet and lay out what I will wear. I go to the bathroom to wash my face and put on some makeup. I return to my room, get dressed, and go downstairs to wait in the lobby for John.

I ask the monitor behind the desk if she has suggestions for a nice place to eat in the neighborhood. She asks, "What are you interested in eating?"

"Pizza, spaghetti, or lasagna."

She says, "I would go to Luigi's. Go to Main Street and turn left. It's about four blocks down. They have huge portions, and the prices are reasonable."

I thank her for the recommendation, go into the parlor, and sit in a chair waiting for John. I look at my watch. It is about 7:32 when John comes in the front door. I get up and go over to him. I put my arms around him, hugging him, but I notice he is not embracing me back. We kiss, but not with any real passion. I know something is seriously wrong when his hands never touch my breast.

I tell him about the restaurant's recommendation, and he says that is fine. We leave and drive to the restaurant. It's a classic Chicago Italian restaurant. We go in, find a small booth in the back, and sit down. The waitress comes over and takes our drink order. She leaves us their menus.

We look at them for a while, then John asks, "What would you like to eat? Would you like to share a pizza?"

"Sure, what do you want on it?"

"I would like cheese, pepperoni, and sausage."

"Do you want your own, or would you like us to share a big one?"

"I'd like to share a big one with you if that's okay."

The waitress brings us our cokes, and she takes our pizza order. We don't say hardly anything. We sip our drinks. He asks, "How are things going at school?"

I tell him how hard it's been already. "I must spend a lot of time studying because I never had many subjects in high school. I enjoy working in the hospital. It is an extension of what I did in my senior year of high school. I am comfortable being there. They give me more and more responsibility." Changing the subject to him, I say, "You will be in your sophomore year at Penn State. Are you still taking core courses, or will you take any engineering courses this year?"

"I have one engineering course each semester. In my junior year, that is when I'll get heavily into engineering."

"Are you looking forward to going back?"

"Yes, I have friends there that I've missed over the summer."

The waitress brings the pizza. We let it cool off a little bit before we dig in. It is good. I'm famished, but John still needs to finish all his half. I can tell that John wants to talk about something but needs to know where to start. I try to help him.

"John, you are the best friend any girl could have. I know that I frustrate you sexually. I am committed to what I want to do and will not risk being pregnant. I learned many things from you about my own body and yours. I can never thank you enough for your patience in dealing with me. If it's all right with you, I think it's essential that we be friends. I want to be friends with no obligations. I want you to return to Philadelphia and enjoy the rest of your time in college with your new friends, both men and women. When you graduate, I hope you will get a great job. I'm not asking you to write, call, or stop by Chicago as you return to Waterloo. If you want to stop by, I'll be happy to see you, but I don't require it."

The expression on John's face is like a giant weight has been lifted off his shoulders. I made it easy for him. All he had to do was say, "I agree. Do you want anything else to eat or something to take back to the dorm?"

"My best friend at school is Marie from Brooklyn, New York. She's Italian. I want to get her a meatball sub."

John says, "Done. I'll call the waitress over and order one to-go. We are both sad and happy at the same time.

We get into the car. He looks at me before we pull out of the parking lot and says, "When you find the right man, and you are ready to give yourself totally to him with no restrictions, he will be the luckiest man in the world."

Life Lessons Learned:

One of the hardest things to do in life is give somebody else the freedom to spread their wings. They truly can become the best version of themself without you. This is true in both professional and personal relationships alike. If you nourish them and they fail, you allow them to fail on their own. And, equally, if they succeed, you should take pride.

CHAPTER 44:

Weekends in the Hospital Are the Best

As I progress through my first year, the schoolwork is hard. I am learning a lot, but the weekends are the best time because I work at the hospital. The evening work sessions should be longer. I can only get a little done in two or three hours. I can do many good things on a shift of eight or ten hours on Saturday, perhaps even longer.

With the longer shift, I also have more chances to mess up. As the months go by, I get more comfortable doing whatever they ask me to do in this big city hospital. But, like the old hospital, the ER rotation will come in my second year, which frustrates me.

I speak to the dean of students and ask if I can get some weekend time in the ER. She looks up my record and sees that I spent the last nine months working in the ER in Waterloo. She considers the recommendations in the file from the head ER nurse. She notices that she happens to be a graduate of St. James and somebody she knows.

She says, "Let me see what I can do, and I'll get back to you."

Time goes on into the springtime, and nothing happens. Each of us has a mailbox where we can stop by and pick up mail anytime during the day or night. One day I checked my mailbox, and there was a note from Sister asking me to come and see her the next day.

I saw her, and she told me she had arranged for my ER rotation to start in the last quarter of my first year. I can only go there one weekend a month. I don't care. I want to be in ER, so I am ecstatic.

Sister tells me that I need to see the ER head nurse. I tell Sister I will see that person first thing in the morning. I find Marie and tell her about my rotation in the ER. We both scream for joy.

She says, "I'm so happy for you. It's what you want."

During the last quarter of the year, we are told to consider finding somebody for a second-year roommate. That person would likely be Marie for the second and possibly the third year. If things don't work out, I could request a different roommate. By the time I finish my first year, I had found out whom I could and couldn't get along with.

One evening, I went over and knocked on Marie's door. She invites me in. I am nervous about the conversation, but I start.

"Marie, I don't know if you've decided or given much thought to a roommate for the second year. I would love to have you as my roommate if you're agreeable. We get along well, have fun, care for each other, and I think it would be a great experience."

She responds, "I was going to give you one more day, and if you didn't ask me, I was going to ask you. So, absolutely. Yes, I would love to be your roommate for the second year."

We hug each other, and then we simultaneously yell for joy. I know who I will spend at least my second year of school with, and that is a considerable weight lifted off my shoulders.

Over the coming weeks, we will notify the administration that we want to room together and ask to see the shared room. Second-year students are on the third floor, and we are told we will be in room 304.

I have not seen my family since I left in August. I have talked to them on the phone every couple of weeks. I miss Thanksgiving, Christmas, and the 4th of July. For the first time, I miss celebrating my favorite holidays. I am told that Chicago has a big 4ᵗʰ of July parade downtown, so Marie and I decide to go. It is a beautiful summer day, not too hot, with bright sunshine and the largest crowd of people I've ever seen.

It is on both sides of the street. They have floats and marching bands and soldiers who march. When we are downtown, we see homeless people on the streets. We see massive lines at soup kitchens, even on the nation's birthday.

In some respects, I feel guilty because I have a room, I have food, I have clothes to wear, and I am getting an excellent education. I am helping people who are sick. What more could a person do?

On July 5ᵗʰ, I go to see Sister and tell her, "I think all of us at the school are incredibly fortunate. We have all the things we need. Many Americans have little or nothing. With so many people having so little, we must create our soup kitchen. All the nursing students must help do the work."

Sister says, "I agree, but with one change."

I ask, "What do you want to change?"

She says, "All the sisters, faculty, and administration must also participate."

I smile at Sister and say, "I agree. Could you get it approved?"

"Of course, I will do that as quickly as possible. People are hurting, and we can help."

Life Lessons Learned:

One of the most challenging things for human beings is knowing when somebody else needs help. Some people have this ability naturally, while others need to be taught. A successful nurse is a person who, when walking into a hospital for their shift, must focus all their attention on serving the patient. If they stay focused, there is less risk of making mistakes.

Sometimes, unfortunately, that mistake can cost patients their lives. Nobody is perfect, but we must work hard every day to be the best we can be.

CHAPTER 45:

End of the First Year

By the time I finish my final exams, I have about four days until my father and mother pick me up and take me back to Waterloo. I have about two weeks before I will be on my way back for my second year. In many respects, the year flew by. Just yesterday, I arrived at St. James. It will take a little time to pack my two suitcases. I will do that the night before I leave.

Marie and I go up to see room 304 one last time before we leave. We will share it on our return. I know that I will miss Marie over the next two weeks. I decide to walk around the campus. It is tranquil, and not many people are out and about. We have a nice park in the center of the campus. It has a good-sized fountain and a beautiful statue of Mary above the waterfall. Several old iron benches are painted white. They've been coated with paint so often that almost all the original casting details are gone.

Marie has already left to go back to New York. She is taking a train, and getting home will be the better part of a day and a half. I notice that very few students are left in the dorm. When we eat our meal, there are so few of us that we sit at two tables. After dinner, I go back to the white bench by the waterfall. As I sit, I wonder what I will do with my two weeks off.

I want to go to the hospital and see my friends. John may be home, and I should have lunch or dinner to see how things went in his second year. If I am honest, I want to know if he has a new girlfriend and if they had sex. A smile comes on my face when I think about how often we almost had sex, but I kept my promise to myself.

When thinking about John, I realize I went without meeting a boy for the whole year. I ask myself, "When did I have time for boys?"

I would work harder at meeting boys in my second year. My mind shifts to my list of things to do. I need to go shopping for new underwear. My mom and dad will be at work all day. So will my sister. And Patrick is probably playing baseball, so I can see him in a few games.

We will have dinner the first night, and I will ask if they are still taking soup and bread to the park. If they are, I could help with that. Then it dawns on me that there is one thing I need to do – sleep.

With everybody gone during the day, I will be alone, and I don't have to be up at any time. I can get up and go to bed when I want. I will have no problem filling my time at home.

The next time I sit on the white bench, I think about my experiences this past year. My brain is so full that it can't hold any newer information. Sometimes I stop, look in a mirror, and smile to see if it looks bigger. All the things I store in my brain are amazing because I don't need to use the material I learned in high school subjects.

My brain has a switch in it. I don't control the button; my brain is in control. When it needs to store more information, it turns on the switch and feeds itself. It has an endless appetite for knowledge. My job is to keep providing it.

I am a very different person today than when I arrived at the school. Things will be different next year because I will spend more time in the hospital working a rotation in the various departments. The rotation process has two objectives. First, we broaden our experience to discover what we like and don't. Second, I need to find out if working in the ER is what I want to do. Working in St. James Hospital is much different than volunteering back in Waterloo. I look forward to all my time in the hospital and the ER.

Before I leave, we are at one table and the last dinner. The discussion concerns women who will not return to St. James next year. There were 50 students in my class. We remind ourselves that six will not be returning.

"Does anybody know why they are leaving?"

Mary Brown says, "I hear that three of them must return home to help their families. One of those is my friend. The family is losing their home. She must go back to try and earn some money to support her family. The other three just decided nursing is not for them."

Life Lessons Learned:

I said a prayer thanking God for allowing me to try and become a nurse. If you are given a gift, whatever it is, then use it. If people need clarification about their skills, encourage them to pray, asking for guidance. Once you find out what you should do, do it to the fullest. I found my gift, and it is to be a nurse. Along with discovering your gift, you must try and help those who have yet to discover their gift.

CHAPTER 46:

Home is Different

My parents leave Waterloo on Saturday morning and arrive in Chicago early Saturday night. They stay at the same hotel where all three of us spent the night when they brought me here last August. We speak on the phone on Friday. They will stay at the hotel and pick me up on Sunday morning outside my dorm at 9:30.

For some strange reason, I am apprehensive about returning to Waterloo on Sunday when I go to bed on Saturday night. I know I am different, but I don't know how much the Depression has impacted Waterloo. I am restless for a while, but I finally sleep. I set my alarm for 8 a.m. I get up, shower, put on my traveling clothes, and eat breakfast.

I finish breakfast at about 9 o'clock, then go to my room to check that I left nothing behind. I need to be sure that I packed everything that belongs to me. I take my two suitcases, go down, and set them outside the front door. I sit on one of the white benches waiting for my parents.

Promptly at 9:30, my parents pull up in front of the dorm. My parents get out of the car to come over and give me a long hug and some kisses. I'm ecstatic to see them. Father puts my suitcases in the car's trunk, and we are off to Waterloo. We go back the same way we went before, but things are dramatically different in many small towns.

I never saw so many houses for sale at one time in my life. It looks like nobody is living in them. Many of the storefronts in the downtown areas have been shuttered. I can see people walking the streets, seeming to have nowhere to go. It's like they have nothing to do but walk.

I ask my parents if this is what Waterloo looks like. My mother responds, "We have not seen rain in a long time. We have dust storms regularly, so the whole town, all the houses, and buildings are covered with layers of dust. The grass is not green. The gardens are struggling to grow for lack of water."

My father says, "Many towns in America are worse off than Waterloo. The people of Waterloo are pulling together to help each other, one day at a time."

We don't say much for a while. My mother told me how much she missed me at Thanksgiving and Christmas. Then she changed the conversation and asked me about my first school year. It's like the floodgates being open. I talked to my parents for probably the next four hours, telling them about what I learned, the people I met in school, and about working in the hospital. I tell them it has been my life's most amazing experience. I say, "I can feel myself growing in knowledge, experience, and self-esteem."

I save the best part for last. We are just outside Waterloo when I tell them I am first in my class. That is the first time I say that out loud. My parents are ecstatic for me. They tell me how proud they are of me.

My father asks, "Do you have things you want to do on your short vacation in Waterloo?"

I tell them about some of the things on my list — the people I want to see, and the most important thing, getting some sleep.

My father smiles and says, "Sleep as much as you want. Two weeks is not much time, but we're glad you're with us."

A few moments later, we pull into the driveway. My brother Patrick sits on the front porch waiting for me to come home. I sent him a note saying I'd like to go to some of his games if he plays baseball while I'm home.

My older sister isn't home yet but is on her way home. It is hard to wait. My father and brother take my suitcases up to my room. I walk through the house, exploring each room as if it is new to me. I am looking around to see if anything is different. It is the same. I need to reacquaint myself after being gone for a year.

We eat dinner, then I go to my room and unpack my suitcases. I sit on the edge of the bed, trying to decide if I should call John. He didn't stop on his way home from Philadelphia for his summer vacation. Is that his way of saying our relationship is over? I make up my mind that I am going to call him. I go downstairs to the hallway, pick up the phone, and dial his number. I didn't complete it because I hung up. I say to myself, *This is stupid. Call him. If he doesn't want to talk, it's okay.*

I pick up the phone and dial through this time. It rings three times, and John answers the phone.

I say, "Hello. I just arrived home tonight for a couple of weeks. I wonder if you want to have lunch sometime."

There is a pause, and then he says, "Well, yes, I'd like you to meet my friend from school, Julie."

"Is Julie your girlfriend?"

Again, a pause, and he replies, "Yes."

I say, "Do you think it's a good idea for you to go to lunch with your old flame and your new girlfriend?"

"Yes, I think you will get along very well. How about lunch on Tuesday at the diner?"

"That's fine. I can't wait to see you and Julie." I say goodbye and hang up the phone. He has a new relationship, and for a moment, I am a little sad, but I quickly turn to happiness for him.

I'm looking forward to having lunch with the two of them.

I go into the kitchen, and my mom and dad sit at the table with a cup of coffee.

I say, "I need to get some rest."

My dad says, "Go to bed. We will see you when we see you."

I go upstairs to change clothes, climb into bed, and quickly fall asleep.

Life Lessons Learned:

There are times in our lives when we face significant changes. It may be saying goodbye to a boyfriend or leaving our hometown. When we move out of our comfort level, we have the most incredible opportunity to grow as a person. I realized I was a different person after my first year of nursing school and that my life would be forever changed because of what I was doing with my life. I had only been home a few hours and was looking forward to returning to school and my new life.

Our ability to look at change as a positive prepares us to deal with change for the rest of our life. Sometimes the difference will be for the better, and sometimes it won't. In my career as a nurse, I lived in many different places. Moving out of my comfort zone to an unknown place is a magnificent opportunity to grow.

CHAPTER 47:

Back to My New Home

I sleep until noon on Monday, get up, shower, and put on some shorts and a sweatshirt. Then I fix myself some lunch and go to the hospital to see my friends. My mom is right about the dust storms. The storms have put a cover of dust all over the town. We have layers of dust and dirt on everything. It makes the city look old, gray, and worn. I go to the hospital emergency room, where I visit some old friends.

Tuesday, I sleep in, but not as late as Monday because I am having lunch with John and Julie. They stop by at noon to pick me up. We go to the town diner. Julie is lovely. She is tall, has blonde hair, and a nice figure — but not quite as beautiful as mine. She is from Atlanta, Georgia, and speaks with a Southern accent. Julie is the picture of grace and poise. We have a nice lunch.

When she needs to go to the ladies' room, she excuses herself, and after she is out of earshot, I say to John, "What about the condom?"

He laughs, but he does not answer my question.

Julie returns, and we all leave. They drop me off at Patrick's baseball game. I sit in the bleachers and cheer for him every time he is at bat, and every time, he makes a great play.

When the game is over, the two of us walk home. I ask him about what is going on in his life. "Do you have a girlfriend?"

He responds, "Sort of."

I say, "What do you mean, sort of?"

"Well, we spend some time together, but we also have other friends."

I ask Patrick if Mom and Dad are still taking soup and bread down to the park. He says, "Every Saturday."

We get home, and when we're into the house, we take some lemonade out of the icebox and go out to the back porch. Mom left us some cookies to go with the lemonade. He asks me, "What is it like to go away to college?"

"Do you mean the subjects I'm studying?"

"No, you left home and haven't returned for a year. What's college life like?"

So, we talk about all the non-academic things I am doing, which isn't much. But he seems curious, so we talk till Mom and Dad come home. I help Mom fix dinner.

I go to a couple more of Patrick's baseball games and go to the hospital for lunch several times. I take one afternoon to walk downtown to see the devastation the Depression has on my hometown. I help my parents bake the bread and make the soup we bring to the homeless at the end of Myrtle Ave. on Saturday. As we prepare the food in the kitchen, I tell my parents that we are starting up a soup kitchen at the college when I get back.

Before I realize it, the two weeks are gone, and it is time to leave. I know that I won't see my family for another year. It would be too expensive for them to come to Chicago to see me. On Saturday morning, I bring two suitcases to the car's trunk. My dad loads them into the car. We are off to Chicago again.

They drop me at the dorm, spend the night in the hotel, and return to Waterloo on Sunday. I put my suitcases inside the front door and check in to get my room key. I can see that Marie is already here. I leave my suitcases downstairs and run up the steps to the third floor to room 304. I put my key in the lock and opened it.

There, lying on her bed, is my best friend and roommate, Marie. She jumps out of bed when she sees me, flies across the room, and puts her arms around me. I give her a great big hug.

"I know it's hard to believe we've only been gone two weeks, but I miss you so much, Marie. Do you want to come down and help me move my suitcases up here?"

"Not a problem."

We bring the two suitcases upstairs. We talked about everything we did or did not do during our two-week vacation. I unpack my suitcases and go over and lie on my bed. I turn on my side so I can see Marie. She turns onto her side so she can see me. That day, we became best friends.

Life Lessons Learned:

One of the strange things about going home is that you must leave another home to get there. So, which one is your real home?

Your real home is where you are living now. Some people dread the idea of leaving home to go someplace else. I will never forget when I told my mother I wanted to attend nursing school in Chicago. She said, "Why can't you stay in Waterloo and go to the local nursing school here?" I tried to tell her I wanted a change. I wanted to see the world. My mother and father were born, raised, and lived in Waterloo, Iowa. For many people of their generation, that's what they wanted to do.

As a nurse, I had many opportunities to work at different hospitals in different cities. I had a sense of adventure. Not everybody can be an adventurer. Life and growing are about experiences, and moving from hospital to hospital can be a very rewarding experience. You can grow by having more than one hometown.

CHAPTER 48:

Year Two, and Men

We sit on the edge of our beds, and I tell Marie, "I need male companionship."

"What?"

"Yes, I have not had a relationship with a man since I left John in Waterloo." I told Marie about my decision to not have sex yet.

She looks at me with a strange look on her face. Then she asks, "Are you a virgin?"

I pause and say, "Yes."

"I don't understand. Look at you. I'm jealous of your body and face, and you have a brain to boot. How is it possible that you have never had sex?"

"You are right. Boys hit on me all the time in Waterloo. But since I've been in Chicago, not once."

"Could it have something to do with the fact that you are in a women's college and have no free time?"

"Have you had any real contact with a man since you have been here?"

"Excuse me, but I think I go to the same school as you, so I have not had any contact with men either. I'm not as smart as you, Miss First in Her Class. I must work harder than you. We have every other weekend off. What happens to our time?"

"Our life has three things — work, study, and sleep. The only time I can remember leaving the campus was last month's 4th of July parade. Things must change this year. We are going to find some male companionship. Are you in?"

"I'm in."

"In two weeks, we have the weekend off. We are going to downtown Chicago and finding some men."

Marie suggests, "There are a lot of other colleges in and around Chicago. We need to find out what is going on at those schools for an opportunity to meet and make both male and female friends."

Two weeks later, we took the train to downtown Chicago. We ask the conductor how to get to Rush Street. He tells us, "Go down to the street, turn left, and go to the first street on the right, then turn right. You'll have more fun and more trouble than you can imagine."

We choose Rush Street because it's the most exciting place to be in Chicago. It is where nightclubs, restaurants, and gangster killings happen. It is unlike any other city in the world.

Finally, we get to Rush Street. The night is a warm September evening, so I take off my sweater and wear the sexiest dress I own. Marie takes one look at me and says, "I have no chance. Everywhere we go, every man in the joint will have their eyes on you. They'll never see me. You're that gorgeous."

She is not jealous — well, maybe a little bit. She thinks I am an attractive woman and knows men will be too. It takes a little time. We enter the bar, sit down, order a drink, and within about a minute, six guys crowd around us.

I can't see which body the hand is connected to that is playing with my butt. I look down and say to him, "Get your hands off of me!"

I say it so loudly that four of the six guys leave in a hurry. The two guys who remain are handsome, tall, and slender. Having not been out with Marie before, I have concerns about how far Marie is willing to go. I know my limit, but I'm unsure about Marie.

We talk for a while, and the man who interests me suggests we all go to dinner. We walk about the block and come across Luigi's Italian restaurant. We go inside and get a table for four. Fred orders a bottle of Chianti. I do not know what it is because I never heard of Chianti or drank any, but I want to try it.

After a few sips of the wine, Fred asks us if we are from around here.

I answer, "Yes, we go to the nursing school at St. James Hospital."

He says, "Where was home before you came here?"

We tell them we are from Brooklyn, New York, and Waterloo, Iowa. I ask Fred, "Are you from Chicago?"

"Honey Bun, I grew up here. I've lived here all of my life."

"You know, Fred, I hear that Rush Street is famous for all kinds of things — good and bad."

"You got that right. If you look out the restaurant's front window, down to the right, I stood there one night and watched a gangster get shot down right there on the corner."

My reaction is, "Really?"

"We've got restaurants and gangsters on Rush Street. We've got casinos and speakeasies. We've got shows and short-stay hotels."

I had never heard that term before, so I asked Fred, "What's a short-stay hotel?"

He looks at me like I just fell off the turnip truck. "Short-stay hotels are for people who only want to stay a short time."

I am still confused. I don't know what that means. Fred thinks momentarily and says, "It's a place where couples enjoy each other's company."

Finally, I get it. Marie is listening to this conversation.

I ask her, "Is there a street like Rush Street in Brooklyn?"

She responds, "Similar to Rush Street, but not anywhere near as exciting.

We finish our dinner, and I look at my watch. It's 9:45, and we must be back by 10:30. "Fred, I know this is weird, but we have to be back at the dorm by 10:30. We have to go get the train back to the college to make sure we're in the dorm by 10:30."

I can see the disappointment on his face that he won't be going to the short-stay hotel with me, and the evening is just about over.

Fred says to both of us, "I have an idea. Why don't we drive you back to the school? That way, we'll make sure you get there in time. Let's go out tomorrow. Do you like baseball?"

I respond, "Yes, I watch my brother play."

Marie says, "Are you kidding me? I'm from the home of the Brooklyn Dodgers! I love baseball."

"The Cubs are playing tomorrow. Would you like to go?"

We look at each other and say, "You bet. What time?"

"We will pick you up at the dorm at noon. We'll go to the ballgame, have dinner, and get you home on time."

We pull up to the dorm with 12 minutes to spare. I get out of the car along with Marie, Fred, and his friend. We give them a simple kiss on the lips. We sit up half the night laughing and giggling about what a great time we had with the boys and how we're looking forward to tomorrow.

Life Lessons Learned:

The excitement about meeting people in a new city is exhilarating. The physical environment can stay the same, but it can appear different when you change the players in the environment. A new nurse or doctor in a medical space can change the dynamics of the people who occupy the space. When you have an opportunity to change the environment for the better, take advantage of that opportunity.

CHAPTER 49:

Back in the ER

Before Thanksgiving, Sister tells me that I will start a rotation in the ER on nights and weekends for at least three months. I am excited because, for the first time, I will be able to drop my anchor in one place for a lengthy period. I flourish in the ER. I make friends with doctors, nurses, secretaries, and custodians. I do everything and anything they ask me to do, and as I advance, my knowledge grows.

This hospital is just a short distance from Rush Street. Patients arrive in the ER from West Chicago and the suburbs around the hospital. The patients in the daytime are dramatically different from the patients in the nighttime. We hear many stories from Fred about people being shot on Rush Street and other parts of Chicago. When I'm in the ER, there seem to be shootings at least once every night. Some of them cause superficial wounds, while other times, the patient dies.

It takes me a few evenings of shootings to realize that the people lying on the gurneys, who are well-clad and groomed, are cadavers. They have polish on their fingernails, shiny shoes, silk ties, and expensive suits but are dead because of disputes over territory, drugs, alcohol, gambling, and prostitution.

When things quiet down, I talk to the doctors and nurses about gang violence in Chicago. One of the doctors says it's all about ego and money. The gangsters have more money than they could ever spend. They're incredibly protective of their turf. If somebody tries to home in on it and take over the businesses they're running, they feel they must defend it at all costs.

One evening at the hospital in March 1932, I come across something on the front page of the Chicago Tribune about death, but it doesn't occur in Chicago. Instead, the crime takes place in East Amwell, New Jersey. One of America's greatest heroes, Charles Lindbergh, and his wife, Anne, have lost their 20-month-old son, Charles Junior. He was kidnapped from his crib. I must've read the story three times, trying to figure out why somebody would kidnap a 20-month-old baby.

The City of Chicago and the country grieve for the Lindberghs and their loss. I discovered in May that the Lindbergh baby's body was found by the side of the road near their house. We grieve for a few days and then return to our daily routine.

When I started working as a volunteer at the hospital back in Waterloo, I will never forget the day I saw a man die in the ER. Several people die on my rotation here at St. Vincent's. Some die of natural causes, and some were by outright execution. By the time I finish my ER rotation, I wonder if the amount of death I've seen hardens me against the pain and anguish of death.

In some respects, people who die of gunshot wounds are just as dead as somebody with a heart attack. The nature of their deaths is medically different. I believe that the time I spend with patients dying of natural causes gives me more peace than treating somebody who is vibrant and alive moments before who is cut down by machine-gun bullets.

Life Lessons Learned:

Little did I know that later in my career as a nurse, I would work feverishly to save the lives of soldiers whose bodies were shot with bullets from airplanes overhead. All soldiers deserve the best treatment to save their lives regardless of the reason. These men decide that they want to fight for their country, and they know the risk they are taking. I understood that I must train my nurses to ensure that every hurt soldier has the best possible care, even if they are clearly going to die.

I want my nurses to be able to walk out of the hospital at the end of their shift, knowing they did their best. They must live with the thoughts of those men. A protocol for a soldier who died in battle is that his immediate supervisor writes a note to the fallen soldier's parents, spouse, or family. Sometimes the leader also dies of his wounds, and a letter must go to his family. The next surviving commander writes a condolence message to the parents.

Many nights, my nurses and I talked about the letters we would send home to the families of soldiers who knew they were dying. These are the saddest letters I ever wrote in my life. They're also the ones I'm the proudest of because I was able to let a parent or a wife know that the last thoughts of the soldier were of family. It does not come naturally for anybody to write a letter for a dying person. Often, the patient knows that they're going to die. They don't know how to say goodbye. One of my accomplishments in life is to help nurses see the signs of impending death and then help them write their letter home.

CHAPTER 50:

Year Two is Done, and I'm Still Number One

Marie and I continue to go out with Benny and Fred. I can tell they are losing interest in us because there is no sex. These are young, solid bucks who are looking for notches on their belts. I'm sure many girls will go out with them and put out for these two guys.

One night, after the boys drop us off at the dorm, Marie and I stay up talking about our dilemma. If we stay with the boys, we must give them more, or the relationship is over.

I tell Marie, "As much as I like Fred, I am not going to risk getting pregnant with one year of school to go. Before I leave for summer break, I will stop seeing Fred. I am fine with you continuing to see Benny, and if he wants more, it would be easier if I am not around."

"Red, I don't think I'm as strong as you. I like Benny, and I think I am willing to take the risk."

To say that I am disappointed is an understatement. It is her life, and I cannot stop her. I can only hope that if she does go all the way, she at least demands protection.

I have about a month of the school year left. I break up with Fred, and Marie stays with Benny. We never talk about what happens on her dates with Benny, but I can tell from the expression on her face that she is having sex. The school year is rapidly ending. I have had another successful year, winding up first in my class again. Marie and I find out that we will stay in the same room for our final year. We ask if we can leave our things in the room while we are gone for two weeks. The administration says it isn't a problem. As in the previous year, Marie leaves first. I have a few days before my parents come.

I started the year by committing to having fun and meeting new people. I met Fred. He's fun to be with, but I realize I must move on. The school year was successful, and I especially loved all the time I spent working in the ER.

Instead of my parents picking me up, my father sends me the money to take the train home and a note telling me that it is less expensive for him to pay the coach train fare than to drive and pay for the gasoline, meals, and hotel for two people. I will be on a long train ride and can sleep on the train. Taking the train isn't a big deal, but I will miss the conversations with Mom and Dad. I have time to walk around campus and go to my favorite contemplation spot, the white bench in the grotto.

I spend a small amount of time looking back at my schooling in year two. The amount of time I spent in the hospital helped me grow dramatically again. We get our class schedule for the third year, and two rotations take up most of the year. The first is the surgery unit. The second is pediatrics. I have been fortunate to see several babies being born over my first two years. Any surgeries I helped with in the emergency room are minor compared to what I will experience in the operating rooms.

The following day, I get a cab to take me to the train station for the ride to Waterloo. I have become accustomed to looking at the newspapers every day. I try to keep up with what is going on with the Depression that has a firm grasp on America. I have yet to read an article of hope. This fall, we have a presidential election. Herbert Hoover is running for re-election against Franklin Delano Roosevelt. Most stories suggest that Roosevelt is a shoo-in because America blames Hoover for the Depression.

My brain needs to catch up getting into Waterloo. My father, solid as a rock, is waiting for me at the agreed-upon spot in baggage claim. He gives me a hug and kiss and welcomes me home. We walk to the car and drive through downtown Waterloo. It isn't possible that things could be worse than they were a year ago when I left, but it is.

I ask Dad, "How are things at work for you and Mom?"

He takes a long time to answer. "Some of the machinists in the shop have been let go. I get all the hours I want because of my experience and specialty machining skill. Your mother's hours have been reduced to about half. If they ask, we can still help the people in the park and family members."

After a pause, he changes the subject to family. "Patrick is playing baseball again. As you know, your sister is engaged and looking to be married just about when you graduate. Have you thought about what you want to do while you're here?"

"Yeah, I want to see Patrick play baseball, have meals with you and Mom, and if it is okay, I would like to help you feed the people in the park. I also want to spend some time with Kelly to talk about her engagement and her wedding plans. But the most important thing is, I want to sleep."

"We will let you get as much sleep as you want and not put any demands on you. It's just good to have you home."

Life Lessons Learned:

In my second year of school, I hit my stride in that I could study and, at the same time, have time for social activities. I think being able to go out with Fred and Benny is what I needed. Marie made me a more balanced person.

This year, I had many firsts — going to a speakeasy, having my first alcoholic drink, and watching a gangster die. When I went into the hospital to work with the doctors and the nurses, there was always talk about how bad things were for many people. Yet each night, I go home to the dorm, eating three meals. I have a bed, clean clothes, and a bathroom with a shower.

This trip back home is the most difficult for me because my home is now Chicago. It is where my life expanded. I became proficient in my skills to be able to help people. Sometimes the best way a person can grow is to leave home and go to another city and perhaps even a different job. Not everybody can do that. The one thing I did consistently that made me better was asking for a transfer or a new assignment. Change can be scary, but it can also be very rewarding.

CHAPTER 51:

I'm Heartbroken

I know something is wrong when I kiss my mother and father goodbye at the train station. All the way to Chicago, I wonder why I have this strange feeling. What could be wrong?

I get a taxicab at the train station and go to my dormitory. I go up to my room, and there is only one name on the door — mine.

I immediately run downstairs to the proctor and ask, "Where is Marie?"

She tells me the most devastating news: "Marie is not coming back."

"Do you know why? What happened?"

She says, "I don't know. I could check with Sister Mary Francis in the morning. She might have an answer for you."

I go into my room and sit on the edge of my bed, trying to figure out what could've happened. Was there a death in her family? Has she been injured? What's the reason why she isn't coming back? Finally, I decided I was going to find out immediately. On the main floor is a pay phone. I look in my notebook and find the home phone number for Marie. I rush downstairs with a handful of change, put the quarters in the phone, and dial her number.

It rings several times before a woman answers the phone, but it isn't Marie. I introduce myself as her roommate, Mary Ellen, and ask if she is around.

The voice, which must have been Marie's mother's, says, "Just a moment."

I hear a conversation in the background, and Marie's mother says, "You have to talk to her." There is a pause, I put in more quarters, and Marie comes on the phone.

I try to be calm when I ask her, "I just found out you aren't coming back. Are you sick, or were you hurt in an accident? Is something wrong with your parents?"

There is a long pause, and she finally says, "Mary Ellen, I'm pregnant. I told Benny, but he's not interested in marrying me. I can't come back to school pregnant."

I am devastated, and I'm not sure what I should say. I can't say, "I warned you," so I ask, "What are you going to do?"

Finally, after a long pause, she responds, "I'm going to have the baby, and I'm going to decide whether to give it up. Then, if I don't keep the baby, I might try to finish school. If I keep the baby, I can live with my mother and father until I find a job to support the child and me. Given the state of the economy, I may be living with my parents for some time."

I don't know what else to say to my best friend. I can't criticize her for giving in to her passions. That wouldn't solve her problem. There is silence between us, and I finally say, "Perhaps you can find a school in Brooklyn that you can return to after the baby is born. You might be able to finish your nursing program there. I know it won't be easy. But with your parents' support, I believe in you and know you can do this. Whatever you decide, please let me know." I told her I would keep her in my prayers. "Please feel free to call me anytime and talk."

I hang up the phone and walk past the proctor. I don't say anything. I go to my room, and I start crying. I know she will never call me.

The following day, I went to see Sister. She isn't in, so I ask for an appointment. I return to my room, sit on my bed, and cry for a while. I need to move on because my classes start on Wednesday. I need to get the books for the first trimester. I stop for lunch even though I'm not hungry. I have a small sandwich, an apple, and tea. After I gather up my books, I make my way back to my room. I drop the books on my desk and sit in my desk chair, looking out the window at the leaves turning colors.

At about 4 p.m., there is a soft knock at the door. Although I didn't hear it at first, the second knock was a little louder. I get up, go over, and answer the door. I open it, and standing in my doorway is a petite woman with simple but elegant features. She is slender and well-dressed. When my eyes meet hers, I see they are like mine — bloodshot from crying.

She introduces herself as Mabel Courts and says she is from French Lick, Indiana. "May I come in?"

"Of course."

She comes in and stands in the middle of the room. She turns around and looks at the whole room. "It is the same as mine."

I introduce myself and ask if I can help her.

"I just found out that we have something in common," she says.

I ask, "What?"

"I found out when I arrived here that my roommate is not returning." Tears start to roll down both our cheeks.

She goes on, "I do not want to spend the last year of school in a room alone."

"I agree. Neither do I."

Mabel goes on. If we room together, we might enjoy each other's company and have fun.

I stop momentarily and say, "I want to think about it. I need to know more about you, and I guess you want to know more about me." We spend two hours talking about ourselves to each other.

The more we talk, the more I'm impressed. I like her a lot. She is very different from Marie. She has her way. I find out that she is number two in our class. We finish, and we decide to go to dinner together. My sadness is going away. I met somebody different, and I like her.

As we go back to the dorm, I suggest we go to my favorite white bench in the garden. We both sit down, and after a moment of silence, I say. "I would like to have you as a roommate, and I hope you want me."

She quickly says, "Yes, I would like that. My room has too many memories of my former roommate. If you agree, tomorrow morning, let's go to Sister Mary Francis and see if we can get a new room for the both of us."

"I agree."

Life Lessons Learned:

In most cases, change can be good, even from painful experiences. Change can sometimes be hard to accept. For some people like me, change can be a rebirth in your life. The relationship with one person may end, but as they say, when one door closes, another one opens.

One of the reasons nurses, like doctors, go through all those hospital rotations is to broaden their skill level. I always wanted to be an ER nurse, but working in different departments in the hospital gave me experience in dealing with people and various clinical situations. I took those experiences back to the ER, and it may take a while, but I'll use all my life experiences.

CHAPTER 52:

Special Surgery

On Saturday morning, I go in early to the surgical floor. I notice there are fewer doctors and nurses on the floor. I go to the nurse's station to ask what is going on when the person at the desk says, "Good. You're here. They want you in conference room C."

Conference room C is the largest of the meeting rooms. I hurry down the hallway, find the room, and open the door. The doctor at the head of the room asks me to come in.

"I think everybody is here, so let's start. We have a 38-year-old male construction worker working on a site on the city's west side. He was on the ground cleaning up debris from the demolition. Three stories above, a structural steel section fell and punctured his head. The puncture stops just short of his spinal cord. A major artery has a puncture, but the piece of steel has plugged the puncture. Our job is to go in and remove the steel fragment, repair the artery, and look for any signs of spinal damage."

The surgeon goes to the blackboard and draws a diagram of what he thinks the injury looks like. He asks the people in the room, "Who should be on the surgical team?"

The first part is made up of the surgeons and specialists he will need. All the doctors are in the room. The lead surgeon says he doesn't know how many people they need. He suggests, and they all agree, that we need two complete teams of surgeons, specialists, and nurses.

The lead surgeon also lists anesthesiologists and the team of nurses. The second team is to be on standby in case the first team needs to be replaced because of fatigue. I have a knack for correctly arranging the instruments on surgical trays, but I'm not a board-certified nurse, so I am surprised that I am asked to watch over the instrument supply.

I can't believe I will be helping in a small way with one of the most delicate surgeries this hospital has ever done. As the meeting adjourns, the surgeons and the specialists move to conference room A to plan the surgery. The head surgeon asks the surgical nurses to join them. The lead surgical nurse calls me over to go with her. She suggests I go to the nurse's station and get a notepad to write down the type and number of surgical instruments they need.

I run to the desk, looking for a notepad. I find one and run back to room A. When I arrive, the surgeon is already talking through a possible procedure. The head nurse tells me what instruments they need and how many should be on the trays. I have several pages of instruments. I go to the head nurse to show her my list to see if I need to include anything. I go to get all the instruments, and when I check my list, the head surgeon says, "We are a go in two hours."

We all go to get ready for this dangerous yet exciting surgery. I search all the instrument drawers in three operating rooms and assemble two sets of trays with all the instruments they say they need. I collect all the used instruments during the surgery and prepare them for the sterilizer. They should be ready to enter the second set of trays. I help the nurses set up the operating room. Secondary personnel like me stand against the outside wall waiting to be told what to do.

After the patient is put to sleep, the surgeon rolls him on his left side because the steel is sticking out of the right side of his skull. He gently moves the steel to try and find out if it is seriously stuck or loose enough to slide out. He grabs the steel with his soft hands to see what happens.

He says, "It doesn't feel like it is in a solid place. Blood spurts out when I move the steel too far."

He makes an incision to open the wound a little more significantly to see if the steel is in the artery or lying on top of it. He can say that the steel has nicked the artery as he pulls back. He stops momentarily and says, "I don't know how big the cut is to the artery. As you know, this artery is the one that supplies blood to the brain. Given its proximity to the brain, he could hemorrhage and die in seconds if we remove the steel."

The surgeons agree to have two clamps lying next to the artery and be ready to suture. The plan is to clamp the artery above quickly and below the puncture, pull out the steel, and quickly suture the opening.

I hear one surgeon say to another, "We have less than a minute to complete the initial sutures. We need just enough sutures to slowly release the clamp to restart blood flow to the brain. We can add more sutures later to fix him permanently."

The surgical team surrounds the body, and everybody knows his job. The lead surgeon says, "We don't have much time. I'm ready to go on the count of three. One, two, three."

He gently but swiftly removes the steel and puts on the clamps. The clamps stop blood flowing and shooting. The other surgeon gets six sutures in place. He is working on the seventh when he says, "Slowly begin to open the clamps."

He continues suturing while the clamps are opened. The clamps are fully open, with just a small trickle of blood. The surgeon quickly sutures the spot where it is leaking.

The surgeons take the steel totally out of the patient's body. As they inspect the impact of the steel, much of the skin is red but not damaged.

As the doctors step away from the patient, they notice his skin color, which is a nice warm pink.

The doctor calls all who are in the room to say to them., "Great job."

A different surgeon comes in and stitches up the wound. All team members leave the operating room. Shortly after that, nurses come in and roll the patient to the intensive care unit.

Left in the room are the nursing students and the cleanup crew. I look at the clock. The surgery started at 2 p.m., and the clock now says 7:30. The tension is so high I'm sure all of us in the room lost track of time. It lasted 10 minutes. As I look back on the procedure, it was very slow and very deliberate. They had to do it that way because they didn't know what they were getting into.

Life Lessons Learned:

The Boy Scouts' motto is, "Be prepared." You never know what can happen.

That suggestion works for doctors and nurses, and it's for all of us because we don't know what will happen daily. Yes, we have predictable activities that occur every day, but how we handle the unpredictable helps define us as a person.

Thinking about what you're going to do before you do it is important. That surgeon could've just pulled out the shard of steel and tried to deal with the result of his action. He did that, but not before planning for all the alternatives. He made a plan that he thought had the least risk for his patient. We shouldn't forget that we risk hurting somebody else if we don't understand the risk we are taking with our decisions.

CHAPTER 53:

Miracle of Life

When I got home from the amazing surgery, I can't remember ever being more tired. I sit down on my bed and just kind of collapse.

Mabel leaves me alone for a while, but then she says, "You must have heard about the surgery today?"

I didn't reply immediately, but eventually, I said, "Yes, I was in it."

"No!" she exclaimed. "You, in it? What was it like?"

"It's the most intense experience of my life. If the surgeon made a wrong move, the patient would've died because he would've bled out in a matter of seconds."

"Are you hungry? Would you like some pizza?"

"Yes."

We go out to a local pizza place and talk for hours about the surgery. Mabel looks at me, absorbing every word that I say. I can tell she wants to be a surgical nurse just as much as I want to be an ER nurse.

My rotation in surgery is over. I am headed to the last rotation in my schooling, maternity. I didn't plan it that way. It just happens, but in hindsight, I'm glad of it. I spend the last five months of my nursing school helping pediatricians deliver babies. We also treat sick babies. The delivery room is dramatically different than the surgical room. Delivery is quiet, while surgery is loud, noisy, and full of people doing other things. The delivery room has a doctor, a nurse or two, and, if necessary, an anesthesiologist. The doctor explained that the baby goes through a great deal of trauma being born. They feel the environment needs to be as quiet as possible.

Of all the things that I've done in my nursing career, watching a baby being born is never old or routine. I only experienced one set of twins being born in my whole rotation. It is impressive how that woman delivers those two babies. Amazingly, she survives it. I can only imagine what it must be like to have three or four babies at one time.

The most memorable time is when couples are having their first child. Everything that is happening to them is a brand-new experience. Every parent would ask after the baby is born, "Is it okay?"

Fathers wait outside in the waiting room, and after the birth, a nurse will tell the father if he has a son or daughter and how the mother is doing.

Not every baby survives. The death of a newborn is difficult for me, no matter how often I see it. The child must struggle to be born. Sometimes death is slow. One day, I stopped at my favorite white bench on my way home. I wonder how Marie's delivery went, if the baby is healthy, and how Marie is doing.

In a very short period, my last year is over, and the exams are done. I come in first in my class, and Mabel comes in second. We both have the exam to get our nurses' licenses. I will return to Waterloo for my sister's wedding and then to St. James to prepare for the exam. I have an extra few days after my finals before the trip home. I make an appointment to go to the employment office of the hospital to apply for a job in the ER. I would interview with the head of personnel. Miss Walters places a note in my mailbox and tells me I will see her three days before I head to Waterloo. The day comes, and I have a 10 o'clock interview for the position.

I go into the reception room and wait to hear my name called. I am a few minutes early. Promptly, at 10 a.m. sharp, Miss Walters comes out and calls my name. I respond, and she asks me to follow her. We walk down the hallway in silence. We come to a door with her name on it; she opens the door and invites me in. I sit in the chair across from her desk.

She sits on the other side and opens the folder in front of her. "You are first in your class for three years?"

"Yes, ma'am."

"You have great reviews from all of your rotations. Would you like to work in the ER at St. James?"

Miss Walters pauses momentarily, then continues, "I would like to hire you for the hospital right now, but your record shows you have not taken your nurse's license exam."

"Yes, that is correct. I'm heading back to Waterloo, Iowa, for my sister's wedding, and then I'll return to prepare and take the exam in mid-August."

"Thank you for that information. I can make you a provisional offer based on attaining your license."

"How long until I find out if I pass?"

"Generally, about two months. We'll hire you as a nurse's aide until we receive notice of the successful completion of your exam."

"Must I leave the dorm?"

"Yes, we have incoming students in mid-August and need the space. I would suggest that you check with the school office and see if they can give some suggestions of places to rent." She stands, extends her hand, and says, "Good luck with the wedding and your exam."

When I get back to the dorm, I tell Mabel what happened.

She says, "I have an interview with Miss Walters tomorrow morning. I hope I get the same story."

"If you do, would you like to room together?"

"I can't think of anyone better. "

Life Lessons Learned:

Someone once said, "Time flies when you are having fun." I couldn't believe that three years had gone by so quickly. I was different due to my decision in my sophomore year of high school. I decided I wanted to do something different, but I needed help to do it in Waterloo. I did achieve my nursing credentials in Chicago so I could go out and dream big.

CHAPTER 54:

A Wedding, an Exam, and a New Life, All on My Mind

I'm taking the train home for my sister's wedding. I leave on Thursday morning and plan to return to Chicago on Monday morning. I have an exam to get ready for. It won't be easy, but my job depends on me passing the exam.

The train leaves for Waterloo at 9 a.m., so I arrive at Union Station at 8:15. I have some time for breakfast before I board the train. I love bagels with cream cheese, crisp bacon, and a cup of black coffee. I look at my watch as I finish my bagel and see it is 8:45, and they will be boarding the train.

The conductor looks at me, and his eyes get wider. That happens a lot just because of the way I'm built. When he regains his composure, he looks at my ticket and tells me I am in the third car from the front of the train. I thank him and wish him a good day. I can hear his response even though he speaks in a whisper. "It's already been a good day."

I go to my car and find my seat. The train pulls out on schedule, and as I sit there, I realize I have nothing to do. My schooling is over, and the study program for the exam will start next week. My attention is drawn to the images I see through my window. As we go through small towns and larger cities, I see plywood on the windows of buildings. Farms and houses have for-sale signs. In some places, out in the middle of nowhere, are shantytowns. The banks have taken back many farms. Nobody is living in the houses or taking care of the land.

Homeless people move into abandoned houses. Some build shelters or live in tents. It has been a year since I came back to Waterloo. It seems even more desperate. I realized that I did have something to worry about. I am going to need a place to stay after I leave school. I must have a job. I don't know how much I will have to pay for rent, utilities, food, and transportation. I don't know how much the security deposit will be for the apartment. All I knew was that I had $25 in the bank. I will have to talk to my parents about some money just as they paid for my sister's wedding.

Suddenly, panic sets in. What will I do if my parents can't give me the money? How will I survive? Then I realized I purchased a newspaper at the train station and put it in my small suitcase. I dig it out and quickly turn the pages until I find at least 100 apartments, which means many more are available that have yet to be listed.

I am looking for apartments close to the hospital. I see at least a dozen. I start scanning the listing for two-bedroom units. There are quite a few, and the rent is between $25 to $30 a unit. With my $25, I could pay half for two months. I will be working and have some income as a nurse's aide. I decided to talk with my parents before the wedding and see if I could borrow $100. I did not ask my parents for money for the entire three years of nursing school. They told me they set aside some money for college. If they didn't need the money over the last three years, perhaps some of that money could help me get an apartment.

I return to Waterloo for the wedding, and the following Saturday is my nursing school graduation. I will ask my parents if they can come to my graduation. With the wedding costs, they may not have the money, which will be all right. I would miss them, but we must make hard decisions in hard times. It's too much to expect them to do both so close to each other.

I might have some money options, so I feel more relaxed. The gentle swaying of the train puts me to sleep. I feel something tapping on my shoulder. I awake to the conductor's voice who says, "Waterloo, next stop, miss."

Life Lessons Learned:

Sometimes change comes at you very fast. You may find yourself needing clarification and support to decide. You must stop for a moment and look at all the challenges in front of you. It is essential to assess each decision to determine the most important ones. As a nurse, when I found myself in multiple crises where I had several patients, I had to assess the most critical and deal with that first. If I didn't make the decision, all the patients suffered because nobody got help.

CHAPTER 55:

The Wedding, and I Ask My Parents for Help

My father is waiting at the baggage claim for me to arrive. I give him a kiss and, more important, a long hug. He takes my bag and puts his arms around my waist as we walk to his car. Before starting the car, he looks at me and says, "Words cannot express how proud your mother and I are of what you accomplished. Thank you for coming to the wedding. Patrick, your mom, and I are coming to your graduation next weekend."

I thank him for his praise. "Your presence at graduation will make it very special to me, something I will remember all my life."

I'm holding back asking him for money now.

"Your Mom has a surprise waiting for you at the house."

"What is it?"

"I'm not saying. I don't want to spoil her surprise."

On the way home, we pass stores closed and shuttered, as well as businesses and homes for sale.

"Dad, is it my imagination, or is there more Depression in Waterloo than when I left a year ago?"

"I'm sorry to say, but you are correct. However, many people hope for Roosevelt and his ideas on how to turn things around. They are calling it 'The New Deal.'"

"How are you and Mom doing?"

"I have a different perspective. They say the unemployment rate is 25%."

"That means 75% of the rest are working doing something. Your mother and I are in the 75%. Things have been more stable in both the shop for me and your mother. So, we are doing just fine."

We arrive at the house, and my sister and Mom rush out the front door.

My sister hugs me so tight I can hardly breathe. No quicker do we separate than my mom steps in for her turn. She doesn't hug as hard as Kelly. It feels good to have her hold me again. We head into the house, and I ask, "Where is Patrick?"

"He is out playing ball. He should be home soon." My Mom takes my suitcase from my dad and says, "Let's go to your room and unpack."

We go up the stairs, and as we get to the top, something looks strange. There is a door at the top of the stairs. I turn to my mom. She says, "Open it."

So, I turn the knob, and a brand-new indoor bathroom is on the other side of the door. "When did this happen?"

My father is coming up the steps and responds, "Last spring."

I stood in the middle of the room and was amazed. It has everything, including a bathtub. "I'm looking forward to a long soak in that tub."

My mother calls me to come into my room. When I walk into the room, a beautiful new dress for the wedding is lying on the bed. "I made it for you using your prom dress. I need to finish it, but it will not take much time to complete. After dinner, I want you to try it on so I can finish it for the wedding."

I look at my watch. "Don't we have a rehearsal dinner tonight?"

"Yes, at 7:30."

"Is what I have on okay for dinner?"

Mom says, "It's fine."

Just about then, Patrick comes in the back door. I hear him shout, "Is she here?"

I yell back, "Yes, she is!"

I hear him climbing the steps two at a time. When he sees me, he almost knocks down Mom to get to me to give me a hug. He has finished high school and whispers in my ear, "I'm going to the University of Iowa on a baseball scholarship. Four years, a free ride."

"What are you going to study?"

He responds, "Civil engineering."

"Wow. I'm so proud of you."

He smiles and says, "How do you like the new bathroom?"

"It's great."

"Have you seen the new kitchen?"

"No!"

We rush downstairs and go into the new kitchen. My mother has a new gas stove, cabinets, and an electric refrigerator.

My father is very conservative with his money. His improvements to the house must have cost a lot of money. I have concerns that he may not have enough money to give me a loan. The worst he can say is no. After dinner, I will look for a time to ask my mom about the loan while she is working on the dress.

We all go to the dinner, and I meet Ted's family. We enjoy the meal. When it is time to go home, we tell everybody we will see them tomorrow.

I go up to my room. Mom followed me and asked if I wanted to try on the dress, and she redid it for me. She wants me down to my bra and panties so she can take my measurements. She pulls out a small notepad she has used for years to write down a woman's measurements.

After taking them, she looks at her notes and says, "Slightly fuller in the chest." Then she says, "How is it possible that I have given birth to two of the most beautiful girls in the world?"

I respond, "Genes." I put on the dress and look in the mirror. "Mom, it's beautiful, but I don't want to detract from Kelly. It is her day."

"No need to worry. She will give you a run for your money in her wedding dress."

I take the dress off, get my nightgown and robe on, and sit beside my mom. I tell her, "I want to talk to you about something important."

"What is it, dear?"

"I will be preparing to take the exam when I return. I must leave the dorm by August 15th. I will not know if I pass the exam until October. I must leave and find a place to live. Mabel, my roommate, wants to share an apartment with me. I will earn some income as a nurse's aide until my report shows that I pass the exam."

My mom says, "So you need some money to tide you over till you can get on your feet and settle in?"

I say, "Yes."

"Your father and I have already talked about what to give you for graduation. We decided to set aside $500. We will give you $100 at a time as you need it. So, next weekend we will give you $100. And as you settle in, you will know you have $400 backup if needed."

I hug my mom and tell her how much I appreciate them helping me.

Mom says, "Your father and I believe in you and that you will help many people in your nursing career."

Life Lessons Learned:

Family is important — not because they can help you when you need money, but for emotional support. I have been fortunate enough to have two families — the one in Waterloo and the family of mankind that I have worked with in my career.

We must treat our families with respect. Some people are not as lucky as I have been. They may not have any family at all. Doctors and nurses work long hours, but I always remind my nurses that they have a family at home and shouldn't neglect them.

CHAPTER 56:

Back to Chicago

The dress my mom made for me fits like a dream; every curve of my tall body makes me look gorgeous, if I say so myself. But when my sister comes down the aisle, she is elegant. It is as if she is floating on a cloud. The wedding ceremony is memorable. We go to the reception in St Mary's Parish Hall, which has been transformed into a mystical place.

I must go home to prepare for an early morning train back to Chicago. I kiss my sister and my new brother-in-law good night and good-bye. My brother Patrick will drive me home and return as the receptionist.

We stop in front of the house, and when he turns off the engine, he says, "Can we talk for a moment?"

"Of course. What is on your mind?"

"Mom and Dad will be all alone in a very short time. Kelly is married, you are staying in Chicago, and I will be off to college in late August. Not only am I concerned about Mom and Dad, but I'm also concerned about what will happen to our relationship. Will we go our separate ways using Christmas cards to keep in touch?"

"Patrick, what would you like us to do?"

"I would like to have all of us meet in a family reunion once a year. It doesn't have to be in Waterloo. It can be anywhere. The point is I don't want to lose contact with any of you."

"Patrick, I'm all for that. When you come to Chicago next weekend, we can talk about it, and you can talk with Kelly and fill her in when she and John return from their honeymoon. Deal?"

Patrick reaches over and gives me a tight hug, and then he says, "Deal."

I leave the car and watch him drive back to the reception.

I enter the house, lock the door, and go to my room. I go into the new bathroom, turn on the lights and stand in front of the mirror. I need to take this dress back to Chicago. If this doesn't catch a man, nothing will.

I get undressed and climb into bed. My sister will never sleep in here again. As I lay there, I think about how much my brother, "The Jock," is concerned about the family. I think about what my parents are going to do about my money problem, and I conclude that I am very blessed to have the family I have.

Before I know it, I smell bacon and coffee and look at my watch at 6:30. I take a quick shower in the new bathroom. How did I manage with an outhouse and wash basin? I get dressed, carefully pack my dress in my suitcase, strip my bed, stuff the bed linens in the pillowcase, grab my bag, and go downstairs to the kitchen.

As I enter the new kitchen, the cooking aroma in the air is similar but not the same. I sit at the table, and Mom sets down a plate of eggs, bacon, and toast. I finish quickly because I am famished. I look at my mom and say, "Things don't taste quite the same. They are different from before."

My dad heard my comment and says, "The difference is, no wood stove. With the wood stove, you had the smokey wood taste that is not there because of the gas burners."

I look at him and say, "You're right. That's it."

My father gets a second cup of coffee and sits beside me. Mom sits across from me. He says, "Your mother, Patrick, and I are so excited to come to Chicago and watch the first person in our family graduate from college."

I must admit, I cry a little, but I tell my parents, "I will be just as proud when Patrick is the first man in the family to graduate from college."

My dad says it is time to go. I kiss and hug my mom and say that I look forward to seeing her next weekend. Just as I go out the door, Patrick comes flying down the stairs, walks over to me, and gives me a kiss and a hug. Just before he lets go, he looks at me and says, "I love you."

Dad and I get in the car and go to the train station. We don't say much in the car. The car stops in the drop-off section, and we both get out. He hugs and kisses me goodbye and says he loves me and will see me in a week.

After the station is out of sight, I start to cry — not tears of sadness but happiness. That weekend, we all said what we all knew but rarely said: "I love you."

Life Lessons Learned:

Our family members knew we loved each other, but until my sister's wedding weekend, we rarely said it. Life is full of many forms of love. When we fall in love with a life mate, that love has lovemaking added to the relationship. We can love our parents and brothers and sisters and even friends. These are all different kinds of love. If someone comes into your life that you like, and they like you, let them know that you care about them.

CHAPTER 57:

New Home and a New Friend

I get back to school, and I have one week until graduation. Mabel is waiting for me at the train station. We stop for pizza and beer before we go back to the dorm. We sit at the pizza place and discuss what we will do with a week off before graduation. I take out the newspaper and show her the apartment near the hospital. We should start looking at apartments first thing tomorrow, and she agrees. I tell her that I am getting some money for graduation. I will have the money to cover my half. I tell her I will get it when my parents and brother come to graduation.

I can see a sad look on her face. "What's wrong?"

"My parents can't afford to come to my graduation, but my father says he will send me money."

"I don't mean to be nosey, but how much will your father send you?"

"He thought about $200."

"That would be great. I'm getting $100, plus I have $25 in the bank, and my father says he will send more if I need it to cover expenses until I get paid." I have a question that will impact what type of apartment we want to rent. "Mabel, do you want to have your own room, or do you want to share a bedroom?"

"That's a great question. We may not work on the same shifts at the hospital, and if we share one room, we may wake each other getting up, going to work, or coming home."

"I haven't thought about that. Our schedule has been the same for the last three years, so the one room worked." We finish our pizza and head back to the dorm.

The following week, we look at ten apartments. We find a two bedroom, in a clean building. It has no furniture, and the rent is $22 per month. The rental is for 12 months, and they want one month in advance for security and the first month when we move into the apartment.

Next, we go to a department store to look for beds, sheets, blankets, and towels. We also buy a few items for the kitchen. We know we will need more, but it's just the basics for now. The week flies by, and my parents and brother arrive on Friday. We have dinner out, and Mabel and I show them our apartment the following day.

Graduation is at 2 p.m. that afternoon. It is small but friendly. I get my diploma, Mabel takes pictures of my family and me, and then I take pictures of my family with Mabel.

Walking back to the dorm, my father gives me an envelope. "Here is your graduation present, plus a little more." There is a lovely congratulations card and four $50 bills.

I give him a huge hug and thank him for being so generous.

We separate, and he says, "Your whole family is so very proud of you."

We go out to dinner that evening, and they drop Mabel and me off at the dorm. My family gets out of the car, and we all say goodbye. I hug Patrick and say, "Enjoy your time at college and get the most out of it you can. Come see me sometime and tell me how you are doing. I love you."

He says, "I love you, too."

Then, they are gone. Mabel and I lock arms and walk to the top of the steps to our room. We go inside, sit on our beds, and look at each other.

I say, "We are on our own."

Mabel says, "No, we have each other."

Life Lessons Learned:

Our lives have milestones in them. One of the essential milestones is when we leave home and strike out on our own to begin a new life. Taking responsibility for one's life is a big and scary step. The more decisions we make, the more comfortable we feel about making other decisions. Practice does make perfect, and making a lot of little choices makes it easier to make big ones.

CHAPTER 58:

The Big Test and the Move

The Monday after graduation, we start preparation for the license exam which we will be taking at Northwestern University. The exam is comprehensive and taken over two days. For a period of three weeks, we spend 10 hours a day in a class preparing for it. During that strenuous three-weeks, I am amazed at how much I have forgotten. As we talk about the exam's various components, the memories come back from the deep, dark recesses of my brain.

We go to school all day, and Mabel and I study in the evenings. The exam will be given Friday and Saturday, and we will not know the results for six to eight weeks. We don't sleep very well the night before big exam. We leave early enough to make sure we are there in plenty of time to sign in for the exam. We each bring a half a dozen Ticonderoga wooden pencils because nobody is smart enough to take the exam with an ink pen.

We go to the exam amphitheater, where I see about 200 nurse ready to take the test. The bell rings precisely at 9 o'clock. I hold my test booklet, fill out all the required information, and stare at the first question. After a while, I still do not have an answer down for the first question. I can't focus. I read the question, but I can't understand it. The more I read it the more I know the answer but can't write it down. I finally say one word to myself, and once I do, I am off to the races. That one word is "focus."

I am the first person to turn in my booklet for the morning session. In fact, I am first in all four sections of the exam, and right behind me is Mabel. At lunchtime we talk a little bit about the first session, and Mabel tells me how she couldn't focus on the first question, just like me. By the time we finish the second session at the end of the first day we are both worn out. We are so spent from the exam that we both take a nap on the train going back to the dorm.

We stop at a deli for a sandwich and soda, sit at the little café table, and I say to Mabel, "One more day and we're done."

When we finish the exam on Saturday, we decide regardless of the outcome of the test we are going to go out and celebrate. We go to Luigi's, and we have wine, pasta, garlic bread, salad, and cannoli for dessert. We are happy, because tomorrow we can sleep and then start the rest of our lives.

We sleep in on Sunday, and first thing Monday morning we move into our new apartment. The landlord opens the apartment door for the furniture and other boxes to be brought to us by the delivery truck. Our first objective is to set up both of our bedrooms. We don't know how the day will unfold, but we want a nice bed ready to get into for our first night's sleep there. Once the beds are made and our clothes are put away, we spend some time dividing the space in the bathroom for our toiletries. The towels and wash cloths are hung on the towel bars, and we say, "Done."

The rest of the apartment doesn't take long to finish. We finish by noon, and we have the whole afternoon off.

We realize that we are both hungry and have no food of any kind in the apartment. We go to the deli for lunch and then to the market to stock the kitchen. While we aren't far from the apartment, we begin looking at all the things we want to buy, and it is more than we can carry. We think about calling a cab, and then we hear a voice say, "May I help you?"

I turn towards the voice and am surprised at what I see. I can tell the man is looking me over. The smile on his face says he likes what he sees. I'm sure he can see the smile on my face when I look him over. We introduce ourselves. His name is Mike O'Grady.

"Do you live in the neighborhood?" Mike asks.

"We just moved in down the street."

"I have my car and I will be happy give you a lift. What is your address?"

"1114 Main Street."

"You won't believe this, but I live in the same building. What is your apartment number?"

I respond, "207. And yours?"

"322."

We load the car, and Mike stops in front of the building. The three of us each make two trips taking in the food and supplies. When we finish, we thank Mike and suggest we should have dinner soon to thank him for his kindness.

We both take a nap in our new beds, and we sleep till dinner time. We go out to a burger joint for dinner. Those greasy burgers and fries taste great.

We both have appointments in the employment office at the hospital the next morning. That's where we find out when we will start our jobs, how much, and when we are going to get paid.

Life Lessons Learned:

Sometimes a lot of important events happen very rapidly, and we don't always appreciate the impact they will have longer-term. Start-

ing a career, moving into a new home with a friend, and making new friends are fun, but what we don't realize at the time is that these relationships may last a lifetime and influence decisions we make many times in the future.

It is easy to live for the moment, which is typical for young people. Understanding the impact of our decisions on our future is hard to understand. It is only after we've gone through these life experiences that we look back on our lives and begin to identify decisions made back then and how they're influencing decisions of today.

CHAPTER 59:

Roosevelt Will Impact My Future

In late September, I receive the notification that I passed the exam. I become a nurse at the hospital December 1st, and I get a reasonable raise in pay. We live more comfortably and put money away in savings. Mabel and I are becoming close friends. She earns her notification of passing the exam the day after mine. So, when we celebrate, we eat and drink too much, but it is still fun. We are real nurses.

The economy is still doing poorly, and the country is still in a depression. In November, we vote for president. The feeling is that Roosevelt is going to win because he offers the people hope for better times ahead. Roosevelt wins the election in an incredible landslide. In the Democratic convention in 1932, Roosevelt has a campaign theme song: "Happy days are here again."

I settle into a routine working in the ER, and Mabel works most of her time in general surgery. Sometimes we work the same shift, but other times, we have totally different ones. There are weeks where we are like two ships passing in the night. The weekends are ours, and we celebrate. I celebrate with Mike O Grady.

We are spending more and more time together. For a while, there is minimal physical contact except on the dance floor. Then on New Year's Eve, 1933, we kiss at the stroke of midnight. Initially, I feel something that I haven't felt since I was with John four years ago. I can see the expression on Mike's face that he is as surprised as I am at the reaction to the kiss. In fact, we find ourselves kissing a lot on New Year's Eve. We go home to our apartments in the wee hours. He invites me to come to his place for a nightcap.

The same feelings I have about not wanting to risk my career when John and I were together in high school are back again. While in high school, I had concerns about risking my opportunity to go to nursing school. Today, I'm just starting my career, and I don't want to give it up so soon. I tell Mike that I will come into his apartment but that the two of us must talk.

He opens the door, goes in, and sits on the couch. It's cold outside, and I have heavy coat on, so I take it off and lay it on the chair. Mike goes and gets us a drink. He sits down next to me and asks, "What do you want to talk about?"

I think about what I want to say before I open my mouth. I tell him, "I like you a lot, and that kiss on the dance floor tonight stimulated passions I have not felt for several years. I didn't allow those passions to take charge back then because I had a concern that the passion would lead to sex and the possibility of pregnancy. I was unwilling to give up my opportunity to go to nursing school for the sake of having sex with someone."

The expression on Mike's face tells me he is in shock.

"I like you a lot, but I just started this journey of being a nurse. I don't want to give it up. It's not that I don't love children. I just want to have a career helping people before I have a career raising children. I never told you that the woman who, for the first two years of nursing school, was my roommate did not come back to the school because she got pregnant. The man who got her pregnant isn't willing to take any responsibility. She had to leave school because she couldn't come back pregnant. She didn't know if she would ever finish and become a nurse. I'm happy to be friends with you. I want to get to know you both mentally and physically, but the relationship must stop at sex. I know you can use condoms, but I also know they can break. If I don't have sex with you, I don't have to worry about being pregnant. So, if you can have a relationship with those conditions, I'd love to be your friend. If you can't, I'll understand. I hope you understand what I'm saying."

Mike sits there the entire time and doesn't say a word. When I finish, I wait for him to say something, and for what seems like an eternity, he doesn't say anything. "I appreciate your candor. You are the most beautiful woman who's ever expressed interest in me. Any man in Chicago would be proud to have you on his arm wherever he goes. If we become closer friends, we may find ourselves exploring each other. There's no question in my mind that I would love to learn more about you. Believe me, I would love to explore your gorgeous body. Somebody once said that when you go on a journey, half the fun is getting there. I don't know how long this relationship will last, but I'm willing to play by your rules. Perhaps, someday, you will change your mind, and let me be clear, if that day happens, I will be ready."

Life Lessons Learned:

The commitments we make help define us as a person. Sometimes, that commitment is to another person, as in marriage, or an employer who's giving us an opportunity to demonstrate our talents and abilities. I look at commitments as promises that need to be kept. If you make a promise to yourself and don't keep it, you will find yourself becoming more and more unhappy. Sometimes the most difficult promise to keep is a promise you make to another person.

There may be a time in your life when you make a promise to someone, and you're wondering, should you break it? Then, you need an objective source to help you make that decision — a friend, priest, rabbi, minister, even a psychologist or psychiatrist can be a great support when making the decision to break solemn promises. Most people cannot make that decision on their own. Seeking wiser counsel will give you comfort regardless of the outcome of your decision.

CHAPTER 60:

Happy Days — Will They Ever Come?

Having my own apartment, including my own bedroom, is a whole different experience than living in my parents' house or living in a dorm. When I want to be with a man, it can be challenging.

After about two months of seeing each other regularly, Mike and I are sitting on the couch in his apartment, listening to some music.

We have been kissing passionately. After we stop and my head is leaning on the back of the couch, I feel Mike's hand unbutton my blouse. I don't stop him. He finishes all the buttons down the front and helps me out of my blouse. He whispers in my ear, "I would love for you to stand up and face me."

I don't hesitate. I stand up, and his hands go around my waist, and he unbuttons and unzips my skirt, and it falls to the floor. He takes my hand and steadies me as I step out of my skirt. He reaches down, picks up my skirt, and lays it on the couch next to my blouse.

He stands up and helps me pull the slip I am wearing up over my head. He lays it next to the other clothes. The only things left on are my bra and panties. He reaches around, and I know what he is going to do. I let him unsnap my bra and pull it gently over my shoulders and away from my breasts. He raises his hand and lays it on my right breast, and he puts his lips on my left breast. I put my arms around his head and let him take as much of my breast in his mouth as he wants.

I let my arms go down to my sides, and he lets go of both my breasts and stands there. "Red hair, green eyes, and the most incredible body I have ever seen."

I'm somewhat shy, and while he is looking at me, I begin to help him undress until all we have on is our underwear. He takes me by the hand and leads me down the hallway to his bedroom. I stop at the door because I know I might well be entering into dangerous territory.

Mike is in front of me, and when I stop, he turns and faces me. "What's wrong?"

"If we go in there and get in bed, we may put both of our commitments in grave danger."

He looks at me and smiles. "I think we can figure out how to satisfy each other without intercourse. I think it might be a lot of fun trying to find different ways. At the moment, I only have one request. I want to get under the sheets, and I want you on top of me with those beautiful breasts pressing on my chest."

I respond, "I think I can do that."

We get in bed and under the covers. I gently climb on top of him. I put my hands on his shoulders and extend my arms straight. In that position, my breasts are just above his chest. As I lower my upper torso and they met his chest I feel a shiver all over my body. His hands come up from his side, and he caresses both my breasts. Next, he pushes me forward so he can reach my breasts with his mouth.

For the next several hours, we explore each other, and then rest only to get enough energy to explore some more. It is the most amazing sexual encounter, and it didn't include intercourse. We fall asleep and spoon, with me in front of him and his arms around me with his hands caressing both of my breasts.

We wake up famished. It is 7 o'clock on Saturday morning. Neither of us must work. We spend another hour just holding each other and occasionally kissing.

Finally, I say, "I'm starving. Let's get something to eat."

He laughs. "I agree, but let's take a shower first. How about together?"

"Okay, then we can talk about what we want to do the rest of the day."

We go to the diner, and nobody is around. We go inside and ask at the counter where everybody is. The waiter says, "Happy days are here again. In about 10 minutes, Franklin Delano Roosevelt will be inaugurated as the 32nd president of the United States."

We had been so obsessed with each other's bodies that we forgot about the inauguration of a new president. While we are eating our breakfast, the conversation first focuses on the adventure of the night before. The experience of exploring each other both physically and mentally makes me wonder, *is this the end or just the beginning?*

I finally say, "Enough about last night. What's going to happen with the new president? What do you think?"

"Given the magnitude of the vote, the American people are looking for serious change. I certainly understand with the Depression why they are desperately looking for something positive to happen. I'm not sure his policies and the things he's talking about doing will bring this country out of Depression." He pleasantly surprises me when he turns to me and asks, "What do you think will happen?"

He asks my opinion about the election and what the president will do to rebuild the country. I pause for a moment, and I know I have a strange look on my face. Mike asks me, "What's wrong?"

I say, "I am astonished that after partying all over my body for most of the night, you would ask me what I think about the country. You pleasantly surprised me when you asked that. I watch what is going on in my hometown of Waterloo, Iowa, and all the towns between there and Chicago every time I go back and forth from home. I see many people have lost their jobs, many farms and houses are shuttered, and many factories are closed. The drought and winds are blowing away our topsoil. I see hundreds of shantytowns where homeless people are trying to survive. I hope and pray that we can find a way to come out of this Depression. Like you, I am unsure as to whether Roosevelt can save the country."

Life Lessons Learned:

I test myself in the arms of another man, naked, except for my underwear. I let him caress my breasts and explore my body as I did his. While it was stimulating and fun, it lacks true fulfillment. The ultimate gift that lovers give to each other is joining their bodies as one.

In all the time I knew Mike, we never had intercourse, but as we thought we were progressing, we found that we really weren't progressing. Within a year, I wasn't half-naked under his covers again. What I was beginning to understand was that my issue wasn't about having intercourse and getting pregnant. It was that I didn't want to give myself entirely to someone else. Until I was ready to do that, intercourse would never be truly satisfying.

I also learned that some people can be interested in what I think even though I have a great body.

CHAPTER 61:

Brutal Winter, and I Lose a Friend

In 1934, things in the country are still bad. Unemployment is 22%. Kansas, Texas, Colorado, and Oklahoma are now a Dust Bowl. Dust storms ruin about 100 million acres, and another 200 million acres of crop land. Things cool down with Mike, and we see less and less of each other.

The famous gangster John Dillinger is shot outside the Biograph Theater, on Lincoln Avenue, in Chicago on July 22nd. The spot is just a few blocks from my hospital. The famous bank robbers, Bonnie and Clyde, are slain in a shootout with police on May 23rd. It always seems strange to me that millions of people follow the movements of gangsters.

Just last year, the mayor of Chicago, Antonin Josef Cermak, is shot while shaking hands with President-Elect Franklin D. Roosevelt at Bayfront Park in Miami, Florida. The newspapers say all the violence is because of prohibition. The gangsters own the speakeasies and make huge profits by selling illegal whisky. I can never figure out, with the economy in such bad shape, where all the money comes from. One day when I am thinking about this, I remember something my father told me: "If unemployment is 22%, that means that 78% of people do have a job."

The number of shootings continues to rise. So does the number of victims coming into my ER. We build a reputation in Chicago as the place to go if you are shot. Mabel's surgery department is also busy because of the shootings.

Late in 1934, I request an interview with my nursing supervisor. I want to talk to her about an idea I have. When we meet, I tell her that in my most recent review, I was told that I should consider going back to school and getting a bachelor's degree in nursing administration. Betty Walker is the head nurse in the ER, and while she does not perform my review, she has a look at it. She agrees.

Some nurses who want to go into management can't afford to quit and go to school full time. They go part-time a few evenings a week and on Saturdays. It takes longer, but you wind up with a better job and more money if you get that degree. She suggests that I investigate Loyola University. Just as I am getting ready to leave, Miss Walker says, "If you give us two years after you finish, we will pay for most of your schooling."

That catches me by surprise. I leave for home and speak with Mabel.

We talk about it for several hours. Mabel says to me, "You are a natural leader. You should do it."

Over dinner, Mabel has something that she wants to talk to me about.

"What is on your mind?" I ask.

"I love living with you, and I love my job, but I've been thinking about what is important to me. I have been living through the brutal winters of Chicago for the last 5 years, and I think I need a change of environment. I want to go to San Diageo and be a nurse in a hospital there if I can find a job. After the first of the year, I plan to start looking there for a job. I don't know how long it will take, but I want to let you know what I'm thinking."

I remember all the bitter, cold winters in Waterloo and coming to Chicago and having even colder winters. "First, let me say, I'm happy for you and I hope you can find what you want in California. I will envy you with no snow or subzero temperatures. Perhaps, someday, I can come and join you?"

Mabel says, "I don't know how long it will take to find a job, but I need a change. I think I have enough experience that I should be able to find one. Applying long distances may be a challenge, but I really want to try."

We finish our dinner and, finally, I say to her, with tears in my eyes, "I will miss you."

She looks at me with tears in her eyes and speaks. "I will miss you too."

We get up, hug each other, and walk arm and arm, both of our spirits lifted at the thought of each of us starting a new adventure.

Life Lessons Learned:

One of the most challenging things in life is to say goodbye to your best friend. Sometimes the best way for us to grow as a person is to let go. When we let go, we open new opportunities for ourselves which challenge us to strive to do better and make us better people. Sometimes other people can see things about us that we cannot see.

Miss Walker saw something in me that made her believe I could train and develop nurses. Her observation changed my life forever. We need people in our life to look at us from a different perspective and dare to tell us.

CHAPTER 62:

This Is Harder Than I Thought

I go to Loyola University to meet with a counselor about a Bachelor of Science in the nursing administration program. How much time would I have to spend on the program?

She says, "If you are working full-time as a nurse in the ER, it's exhausting to try to go to night school. It can wear you down."

We talk about a good time for me to complete the course work. She responds that classes are an hour and a half during the week, and five hours on Saturday.

I ask, "How many days a week do I need to finish the coursework in a year and a half?"

"If you go three nights a week and five hours on Saturday, you could finish in a year and a half. If you go one night a week, it will take you two years. That's what most people opt for. It's hard, but not impossible."

If I start in September 1934, and take the three nights a week schedule, I will finish in January 1936. The hospital is willing to pay my tuition and fees in exchange for successfully completing the courses and giving them two additional years working at the hospital. I would be supervising nurses, but there's no guarantee that I would be supervising in the ER.

Two more years after completion, I could apply for nursing administration jobs. That would take me to 1938 and would mean I'd have five more winters in Chicago, and whatever social life I could have would be absolutely on hold for two years.

I ask when my application must be in, and she replies, "June 1st, so you have several months to make up your mind."

I thank her for the time and the information she gave me, and I leave to go back and talk with Mabel and see what she thinks.

I walk in the door, and Mabel is reading a book. I sit on the couch next to her.

"May I ask you a question?"

"Sure."

"I was just in the admissions department for the Bachelor of Nursing Management at Loyola University to investigate their program. If I go three evenings a week and five hours on Saturday, I could complete the program in a year and a half. Although the hospital says that they will pay my tuition and fees if I successfully complete the course, I will owe them two years of work in the hospital. You know I hate the winters in Chicago as much as you do. If I want to do this, I would be looking at five more winters in Chicago. I don't have the money to quit my job and pay the tuition and fees out of my savings."

"Could you ask your father for the money?"

"I suppose I could, but it just doesn't feel right. I'm a grown woman, I have a job, and I'm taking care of myself. I wouldn't feel right telling my father that I want to quit my job and depend upon him not only for living expenses but also ask him to pay my tuition and fees. I don't think that's an option."

Mabel says, "Well, you don't ask for much."

"That's true, but things are still terrible in this country, and my mother or father could lose their jobs at any time. I wouldn't want to burden them with my additional expenses."

"I will tell you again that I think you will be a great nurse administrator, and with that on your resume, you can go a lot of places. I've been thinking about our conversation about me moving to California. I still want to do that, but I have concerns about the Depression. I would not want to go to California without a job. What I can do for you as I look for work is give you some idea of how the prospects for the job market are in California. If I can't find a job right away, I'm staying in Chicago, keeping my job at the hospital, and staying with my best friend. I am speaking selfishly now. If you take the three days a week path and I'm still here, we will have less socializing time together. So, being selfish, I would like to see you do it two nights a week instead of three. Whatever you decide, I'll support you. I want to make the best of whatever time we have together."

We stand up and hug each other. I say to her, "You're a great friend. I'm glad you tell me what you really think. I am glad that I have a friend I can talk to about what I want to do. When I make up my mind, you'll be the first to know."

After about a month, I decide that I'm going to try the three nights a week. So, I enroll in the program and start my night classes in September. When I start my classes, Mabel is still with me in Chicago. Mabel receives a letter in November containing an offer of a full-time nursing position at Scripps Mercy Hospital in San Diego, California. She would have to be there on February 1st, 1935.

She is alone when she gets the letter because I usually go from the hospital directly to classes on Monday, Wednesday, and Friday. I usually get home around 9:30 at night. When I step in the door, she jumps up and grabs me in her arms.

She yells, "I'm going to California!"

We sit on the couch, and we read the letter three times. We are both ecstatic and sad at the same time. We celebrate Thanksgiving and

Christmas together, and she leaves in mid-January on her adventure to California.

I go with her to the train station. When I return, I realize I will be all alone in my apartment. I continue my studies three days a week and Saturdays. I think several times about trying to find a new roommate. By the time I finish my schooling, I am very comfortable living alone.

I go out with some men that I've met at work or at school, but there is nothing serious. The relationships are more social than anything else. At the end of June 1936, I complete my advanced degree, and my parents come to my graduation.

Life Lessons Learned:

If you look back at your life, can you remember all the milestones you hit? When you decide to change your life, whether it's relocating to another city, or a new job, or advancing your career with education, it's perfectly natural to wonder if you made the right decision.

Mabel made the right decision for her life based on the quality of life she wanted. On the other hand, I wanted to advance my career in nursing. Both were the right decisions.

CHAPTER 63:

Things Are Still Difficult

While I am working and going to school in 1935 and 1936, the Depression continues. Unemployment hovers around 21% for the third year in a row. Pres. Roosevelt creates The Work Progress Administration (WPA) and many other programs run by the government to put people to work building infrastructure in the United States. The WPA employs over 9 million people and costs over $11 billion.

In August 1935, President Roosevelt endorses the Neutrality Act, which stops the exportation of war items like arms and ammunition from the United States to any other nation that is at war with America. Unfortunately, many people see this act as making America an isolationist nation. In addition, the newspapers are reporting the wave of fascism that is sweeping across Europe.

Mussolini's Army invades Ethiopia to expand the Italian empire. They want to take the capital of Addis Ababa. After the surrender of Ethiopia, there is talk in the hospital that there is a possibility of war in Europe. However, because of the Neutrality Act, the consensus is that America will not be in another European war.

With all the uncertainty, the continuing Depression, and a possible war in Europe, I decide to distract myself from all the negative thoughts. So, I take some money and buy an Atwater Kent radio. I have always loved music, but I know I wouldn't have the money to buy a record player and an endless supply of records.

Shortly after I get my radio, I find a program called the "Lucky Strike Hit Parade." It is a one-hour radio show that plays the 15 most popular songs that week. The show changes the top 15 every week and airs on Saturday night. So, with my schedule, I can go to school, go home and study, fix myself dinner, and then sit down and listen to "Your Hit Parade."

Another one of my favorites on the radio is the Green Hornet. I also like to listen to Bing Crosby in the Kraft Music Hall. I think the most memorable radio show I ever heard takes place on December 11th when King Edward VIII of England speaks to the world from Windsor Castle, explaining his reasons for abdicating his position as king of the British Empire. Sometimes I can hear a broadcast from Europe and hear the news of what's happening there.

It seems like there is a new radio show every week. The shows are a great distraction from work, study, and the Depression. I know the characters on the shows as if they are my friends. The stories never end; they continue from week to week. I sometimes feel myself rushing home because I don't want to miss The Goldbergs or Backstage Wives.

I wonder what I filled my time with before I bought the radio. I don't care. I really enjoy listening to my radio.

Shortly after finishing my schooling, I realize how much free time I have. All I need to do is figure out how I'm going to fill it. In January 1936, I am in the library at Loyola, and I see this man studying me. I still have my figure and, of course, my red hair and green eyes.

When I turn to look at him, he doesn't blink. He just keeps staring at me. I look away, and the next time I turn to look at him, I can see him walking towards me.

"May I sit down?" he asks.

I pause for a moment and look at him. He is quite attractive, so I say, "Sure."

"I don't mean to be bold, but I must tell you that you are one of the most striking women I have ever seen in my life. I just need to come and get a closer look."

I blush and somewhat sink my head in embarrassment. Then I say to him, "You're not bad looking yourself." I can see the shock on his face.

We both chuckle, and then he says, "Would you join me for a cup of coffee?"

I stop for a moment. It has been a long time since I've been in the company of a good-looking man. I need this, so I say, "Absolutely."

We leave the library and go to a little coffee shop around the corner. We sit down, and the waitress comes over and takes our coffee order.

She asks us, "Anything else?"

"How about a variety of donuts? Is that okay with you?" he says.

I reply, "I can't remember the last time I ate donuts. Sounds good to me."

"I don't know your name."

"I don't think I gave you mine, so I'll start first. My name is Mary Ellen Murphy."

He says, "Well, Mary Ellen Murphy, my name is James Adams Wilson."

He asks me what I do, and I tell him about my job as a nurse and what I do in managing a team of nurses. "And you, Mr. James Adams Wilson, what do you do?"

"I work for the government."

"What kind of work do you do?" He pauses and doesn't reply, so I ask again, "What kind of work do you do for the government?"

"I can't really tell you because it's a secret."

"So, how do I know you actually work for the government?"

"I want to show you something, but don't say anything, okay?"

I say, "Okay."

He reaches into his back pocket and pulls out his wallet. He opens it slightly so I can see a gold badge that reads Federal Bureau of Investigation. I lean over and whisper to him, "You work for the FBI?"

"Yes," he says quietly.

"What do you do for them?"

"It's a secret. I can't tell you, so please don't ask anymore."

I develop a preoccupation with trying to get this man to tell me what he does for the FBI. But unfortunately, it isn't going to happen today. Instead, we are going to have to spend more time together so he can trust me enough to tell me his secret.

Life Lessons Learned:

It is important to be aware of other things that are going on around you. You must have the ability to collect information, store it, and then eventually process it into a usable format. Every day when I went to work or school, not only was I learning from the textbook, but also I was learning at my job in the emergency room. I became proficient at understanding how people think and act, and I use that to make myself a better leader.

Sometimes we run into obstacles that frustrate and intrigue us. I couldn't possibly follow all the things that were going on in Europe, but I tried to learn as much as I could. Each day we can learn something new, and those people who grow the most are the ones who observe what's going on around them.

CHAPTER 64:

I Want to Know His Secret

Over the next three months, James and I spend a great deal of time together. We go out to dinner at some of the best places in Chicago. Sometimes after dinner, we go dancing or to a movie. The formality leaves. I call him Jim, and he calls me Red because of my bright red hair. I am happy, and up to that point, we had no intimacy, which surprises me because I can tell by the way he looks at me he wants me.

We go out to dinner, and he says to me, "We must leave here and go someplace more secure, and then I will tell you why. You have been bugging me to tell you what I do at the government. I'm ready to tell you and ask you for help, but not here. We can go to your place or mine, it doesn't matter. We just cannot talk about it here. What is your choice?"

My mind is spinning with what I think he might want to talk about, and after a few moments of saying nothing, I say, "My place."

Jim pays the bill, and we grab a cab to my apartment. We go in, take off our coats, and Jim walks over to my kitchen table to sit down. I cross the room and sit across from him.

He begins, "Red, you know I work for the FBI, and I want your help in an investigation. I have been working on it for some time in the organized crime unit. We believe that the Chicago mob may be sending weapons and ammunition to Mussolini to resupply his army and expand his influence in Africa. My assignment is to find out if they are. We want to know who is doing it and how they are getting the supply out of the country. These activities, if true, are in violation of the Neutrality Act. My mission is to pose as an arms dealer who has interest in selling munitions to the mafia, who can then send the weapons to Italy."

I'm sitting across the table in amazement. If I could see me, I think my mouth would be wide open. I want to take my makeup mirror out of my purse and check.

"Jim, isn't that an incredibly dangerous assignment?"

"Yes, and I know this is going to sound strange. It's more dangerous for me by myself."

"I don't understand."

"I'll explain. I want you to consider working with me as a civilian to try and break up this illegal supply network."

"I don't know anything about law enforcement. How can I help you?"

"I'm glad you raise the question. Please don't take this the wrong way, but I want to use you as a distraction."

"I don't understand what you're saying."

"The mob leaders always have gorgeous women around them; they're just for looks. You know, eye candy. Other times, there are serious relationships between bosses and women. Right now, I just have me, and I've been looking for someone striking enough to distract the bosses during the conversations. I think, with some work, you could be the distraction that I'm looking for."

I don't know if I should be offended that I'm someone he could work on to make me attractive enough to be a distraction, but I just say, "What do you mean 'with some work?'"

"First, you would need a new wardrobe, new makeup. Everything will be done to enhance and emphasize what you already have. I want to take all of your assets and display them in such a way that their presentation will distract the mob bosses from focusing on the issues at hand."

I listen to what he says, and my first reaction is, "Do you want to dress me like a whore?"

"No, I don't want to make you gaudy. I want to make you glamorous. I want you to look like a movie star. When you walk into the room, I want every head turn to focus their attention on you, not me. I want to hear whispers like, 'Who is that gorgeous woman?' and, 'Why have I not seen her before?' I want to make you look as beautiful as Carol Lombard. I want every man to hate me for having you no matter where we are. I do not want to change your hair color. The combination of red hair and green eyes sets you apart. I know you have ample assets and curves. We just have to bring them out."

I think about all the things he is telling me. The intrigue about working with him in a government operation is exciting. I know I have an interesting body, and the idea of emphasizing the parts doesn't bother me. A few things do concern me.

"I must ask you some questions. Being among all these mob leaders, what's the possibility of both of us laying on marble slabs in the morgue of my hospital before we're done? The second question is, how long will we have to keep the charade up? And the last question is, how do we exit this operation without being slain?"

"These are all great questions. I'll do my best to answer them. There is always a possibility that something could go wrong. The more likely scenario is that I get shot. They will keep you alive for their pleasure and entertainment. When they're tired of you, they will either sell you, often to slavery, or kill you."

"Well, those are scary thoughts."

"Let's move on to your next question, how long do we have to keep this up? If we get into their inner circle, it might take up to a year, so if you sign on, I want you to make a commitment for 12 months. As to your last question, the plan is to negotiate to sell a large inventory of weapons and ammunition to be paid in cash upon delivery to a warehouse somewhere in Chicago. There are, of course, no weapons from our side. The promise of delivery when the money transfers from mob to me is in cash. The transfer area is where the meeting takes place. FBI agents will surround us, and on my signal, they will burst in and arrest everybody, including us, and charge all those caught to be in violation of the Neutrality Act. Once the arrests are complete, your job is done. You don't have to testify. You're out of it. I want you to take some time to think this over. I will understand if you say no; I will not pressure you to do this. I also hope that we can continue as good friends and see each other. Of all the women I know, you appear to be perfect for this role. If we are successful, you may save thousands of innocent people — men, women, and children — from being slain by Mussolini's Army. I want you to understand that if you say no, I will respect your decision."

"Do I have to give up my job at the hospital? I have no interest if I have to do that."

"I can't promise that there will not be times during the day I may need you. Most of the time, I'll work around your schedule to have our meetings in the evenings and on weekends. Red, I'm thinking now that I'm here, you have that big, empty couch. What do you say we go over and play around for a while? Perhaps that will take your mind off the decision you're going to make."

After a long pause, I say, "I don't know how good I'll be with all the things you've given me to think about, but I'll give it a try."

Life Lessons Learned:

Some people say that life is like a curveball that nobody knows the direction of. A curveball usually requires us to do things that we've never done. The first and most important thing to do when a curveball comes at us is to try to assess the risk we would be taking. Firefighters, policemen, and soldiers swing at the curve ball as they risk their lives for the greater good. When the curveball comes to us, can we commit to swing and knock it out of the ballpark?

CHAPTER 65:

Is Carson, Pirie, and Scott in My Future?

For the better part of the week, I think about what Jim is asking me to do. I see him on Friday night, we talk about my decision, and I tell him that I'll to do the best I can.

"If there comes a time when I'm genuinely fearful for my life, I'm going to run away. That's the only way I can do this, Jim. So, if you can live with that, then we're on." I put a smile on my face and ask, "When do I go for my makeover?"

"I'm so happy you are going to work with me. I will make a standing appointment for you for the next four weeks in the woman's department at Carson, Pirie, and Scott to begin selecting a wardrobe. You also have a separate appointment in the make-up department two hours later. The sooner we get going, the quicker the transformation begins and the quicker we get bad guys."

He reminds me that I can't tell anybody what I'm doing. "We must keep a tight lid on this project. You know that more than anybody else. Now, I have a very unusual request."

I look at Jim and say, "What now?"

"May I look at your wardrobe? I need to see if there's anything that I think we can use to support the image or if we are going to have to do a total rebuild. By the way, do you have a plain white long sleeve blouse?"

"Doesn't everybody? Why do you ask?"

"I want you to go put it on without a bra?"

"Why?"

"Most of the clothes for evening wear that are popular today for women do not require a bra. I want to see how you fit into a plain white blouse."

I leave the living room, go back to my bedroom closet, find the white blouse, take off my bra, and put on the blouse. I look at myself in the mirror. I am happy with the look in the blouse. I walk out to the living room and stand in front of Jim, spinning around so he can see me from all sides. "Do you like what you see?"

"Only one word to describe you: perfect. I can't wait to see you in your new wardrobe."

Jim has a smile on his face. I know he is going to say something. All I can do is wait and see what he says. "Red, I'm thinking, when we were on the couch a little while ago, as I recall, you seemed to enjoy that experience."

"Yes. What's on your mind?"

"How about we go back to the couch, and I practice unbuttoning your buttons?"

Here I am again, with another man who is offering me the scariest and most exciting opportunity so far in my life. Am I going to have to tell him, "Jim, no intercourse," or see if I can control a situation without telling him?

"Before we walk over to the couch and pursue your training, you need to know that I'm in charge of my buttons. We must understand the ground rules. I apologize for not telling you them before the last encounter on the couch. And what I'm about to tell you may impact your decision to want to work with me. But you must understand these are the ground rules, no exception."

"Okay, Red, let me hear them."

We go to the couch, and I say, "You can play with my buttons, but we can never have intercourse. I do so for two reasons. One, I do not want to get pregnant, and two, I do not want to change my career as a nurse for now. Someday, I hope to get married, and have intercourse with the man I love. My values come with being brought up Irish Catholic. So, it's up to you. What do you want to do?"

"I want to make sure I get this straight. The only limitation in what we do in our relationship is no intercourse?"

"That's it. For most men, that is a big limitation and turn off."

Jim develops a big smile on his face. He says, "Can I count the buttons first?"

"Yes, but you can't touch until you agree. If you try and force yourself on me, you will pay a price. We will be done. I go, and you're on your own."

The look on his face tells me he believes I am serious. He wants to capture these bad guys, just as much as he wants intimacy with me. "I promise."

"Count away."

"I see nine buttons, seven down the middle, and one on each side."

I look down and see my nipples are showing through the blouse. We walk over to the couch, and he starts unbuttoning all my buttons. When he is done unbuttoning, he leaves the blouse fully open. He reaches inside the blouse and takes a handful of my right breast and, at the same time, kisses me on the lips. With his lips on mine and his hand on my breast, I find myself quivering with excitement.

Life Lessons Learned:

Sometimes we are faced with a situation that we have never been in before, and the process of deciding what to do is daunting. Not everybody is faced with choosing to be a spy for the FBI and perhaps risking their life to save others. Yet, in our everyday life, we may be faced with life-and-death decisions. It may be a family member, friend, or person we have just met, and they need us to take the responsibility of making that decision for them.

It's hard to have values and to stick with them. Passion is a powerful influence, and we have a choice. Do we try to control them, or do we let them control us? Every time the value system we have is challenged, we must decide. Do we reaffirm what we believe, or decide to abandon it? Once we surrender our moral belief, we can never get it back. A decision made in an instant can change us for the rest of our lives. When we are forced to question our principles, we must seek support from the Lord.

CHAPTER 66:

That is Not Me

The next morning, Jim picks me up and we go for lunch down the street from Carson, Pirie and Scott, and we talk a little bit about clothes. But the thing that concerns me the most is the makeup. If I dramatically change my makeup or change something like the shape of my eyebrows, I'll look out of place in the hospital, so we must use makeup subtly to change the look of my face. Since we are the preferred hospital for gang land shootings, I don't want to have a patient or his companions in my ER recognize me. I keep that in mind when we meet with the makeup people.

"Red, are you ready to go?"

"Yes, I think so."

We go in through the big revolving doors, go to the information desk, and ask for lady's eveningwear. The person tells us that it is on the fourth floor. We walk over to the elevator and take it up to the fourth floor, where we see a receptionist, which I think is strange.

I go over to her and say, "I'm Miss Murphy, and I have an appointment at 2 o'clock."

She checks her calendar and says, "Yes, you do." The receptionist signals two young woman to come and escort us to the fitting area.

We are introduced to Madam Wilshire, who is going to be our consultant. She is an amazing-looking older woman. She is dressed impeccably using colors and styles that work with her age and her physical assets.

She asks me, "Miss Murphy, what are you looking for?"

I respond, "I need sophisticated and elegant eveningwear that you might see on Carol Lombard."

"Please follow me to the dressing room."

She goes behind the curtain while I strip down to my underwear. She returns and says, "I can see right now that your bust is much larger than Carole Lombard's, and so we must be concerned about picking eveningwear that will keep your breasts restrained. We don't want them falling out when you move. You have a lovely, well-proportioned shape — a little top heavy, but you carry it very well. You will look magnificent in some of the gowns that I'm thinking about. Put on that robe, and let's look at some gowns."

Madam Wilshire takes me over to a rack of long, flowing evening gowns. She says, "With your red hair and green eyes, we will start with the pure white satin dress with thin straps. Then we should also look at a black dress with a form fitting shape and a deep plunge in the back."

I put on the white one, turn around, look in the mirror and say, "I don't recognize that person."

Madam Wilshire says, "Miss Murphy, that person has always been there, you just never let her out until today."

I go out to the floor, and when Jim sees me the only word he says is, "Unbelievable."

He asks me to walk back and forth in front of him. Then I walk over to him, knowing how low cut the dress is, lean over so that he can look down the dress and see more of me. He says to me with a smile on his face, "You learn quickly. That's some figure you have there. I'm sure it'll work well for us."

I go back and try on the black dress. It gets the same reaction. Jim tells Madam Wilshire, "We will take both of those. We will need underwear and stockings, but we don't need any bras."

Madam Wilshire responds, "She is remarkable!"

Jim asks her what else I should have in terms of clothing and Madam Wilshire says, "She is going to need some casual clothes, skirts, pants, blouses, and jackets."

Jim says, "We have an appointment in the makeup department, so can we come back and look at some other clothes after we finish there?"

"Of course. Just look for me when you get back. If I might suggest, make sure the makeup doesn't cover up her natural beauty. Let the red hair, green eyes, and soft skin be the focus. I would suggest you try different shades of red lipstick to see how they complement her."

We don't spend a lot of time in the makeup department because the makeup person agrees with Madame Wilshire. We work a little bit on eyebrow pencil and mascara, and we find a great shade of red lipstick called "Heat." I am comfortable that I can change the makeup and not risk being recognized in the ER.

We go back to the lady's department, and Madame Wilshire has everything laid out that we talked about. It all looks spectacular. She suggests I go in and try everything on while she rings them up so that Jim can approve. It takes the better part of two hours for me to go through all the clothes, but everything fits, so Jim says, "Pack it up."

We must have someone help carry all the bags down to Jim's car.

We finally get to my apartment and put everything away, then we go back to the kitchen table.

"There is just one more thing I need to talk to you about, Mary. I can't tell you when or where we will have you make your first appearance. You need to be ready on a moment's notice. When I know, I will tell you whether you should dress for evening or daytime. Just in case I didn't tell you, all these clothes are yours regardless of what happens. The other thing is that, for being on standby and the commitment you're making for the next 90 days, you will be paid five dollars a day regardless of whether you do anything. When I first saw you in the library from a distance, I had to see how beautiful you were up close. I had to gather my courage to get up and see you face to face. Again, today, I didn't know what to expect when you came out of the dressing room in that white dress. When you walked back and forth, it was an amazing sight. Then you bent over, exposing a good portion of your breasts to me with no inhibitions and looked straight into my eyes, even when my eyes wanted to see what was in front of them. It was then that I knew you are perfect for the job, and you are going to dazzle the mob."

Life Lessons Learned:

Most people don't know what talents they have deep inside of them, and in many cases, it is never released. Sometimes people take a chance and release it, and in so doing become a different person. Sort of like Dr. Jekyll and Mr. Hyde. You may get a taste of some of the things that are different in you, and having tasted the new you, it turns into an insatiable desire for more.

CHAPTER 67:

The Call

Jim and I spend a lot of time together, some on the couch and sometimes in my bed or his bed. I ask him why I haven't been invited to a party.

He says, "I'm working on it. I'm hopeful we will soon have a place to show your talents. We are making progress in identifying the parties who are involved in smuggling the weapons to Italy."

A week later, around 5 o'clock, I get a call from Jim saying, "I'll pick you up at 7:30. Wear the white dress. It's your turn to shine."

I put on the dress and my new makeup, go look in the small mirror on the wall, and practice bending over. I look to see how far I can bend without my breasts falling out of the dress. A couple of times, one or the other does come out if I bend over too far. I am comfortable that, at about 45 degrees, plenty is exposed but they are restrained. I go down to the lobby a little ahead of time because there is a full-length mirror on the wall. I open my coat, and for the first time since the department store, I get the full view. I do the 45-degree bend, and there they are in full view. I can't believe that I am looking at the girl from Waterloo.

Promptly at 7:30, Jim pulls up in front of my apartment. He gets out of the car and goes around to open the door. He gives me a kiss and asks to see the dress. I open the coat, give him the 45-degree bend, and I hear him say, "Oh my God, how do they stay inside?"

I respond, "Practice."

I get in, and we are off. I ask where we are heading and he says, "The Blackstone Hotel. We have a private party room, and we are meeting Vito Lastra. He is the mob's gunrunner, and he oversees shipping weapons and ammunition to the Mussolini government. In the trunk of my car, I have a small suitcase that has $1 million in it. I will strike a deal with Lastra, and when he takes the suitcase and opens it to inspect the money, one of the waiters who is an FBI agent will signal the rest of the team that the deal is going down. The team will break into the room, guns pointed, and tell everyone in the room that they are the FBI and that everybody in the room is under arrest, including you and me."

"Wait a minute, I'm not going to be arrested!"

Jim says, "Don't worry. Everybody in the house will seem to be arrested, but you and I will be released, and Vito and his friends will be put in jail."

We arrive at the Blackstone Hotel. The doorman opens the door for me, and Jim gets out. He gets his suitcase out of the trunk, and we stroll in. Jim asks the receptionist for Mr. Lustra's dinner party.

"It is on the second floor in the Manor Room. Take the center staircase and go up to the second floor, or you can use the elevator, whichever you choose."

Because of the weight of carrying $1 million, Jim says, "Let's take the elevator."

We get in, turn, and face the door. He takes my hand in his and says, "It's your time to shine. Just be calm, gracious, and most important, flirtatious."

When the door opens, we see a sign on the wall that shows the Manor Room is to the right. We know that we are almost there when we see guards on either side of the door going into the Manor Room. They stop us and frisk Jim to see if he is carrying a weapon. I stop, open my coat, and say to one of the guards, "You want to frisk me?"

That brings a smile to the guard's face. He doesn't touch me but holds the door for me to go into the room.

We go into the room, and a coat check girl asks if she can take our coats. She also asks Jim if he wants to check his suitcase. We give her our coats, but Jim keeps the suitcase, and within seconds after I take off my coat, you can see every head in the room turn to look at what just walked in.

Jim leans over and whispers in my ear, "Look straight ahead at the short, middle-aged man heading directly for you. That is Vito Lastra."

Vito arrives, takes both of my hands, and introduces himself. "I'm sure you hear this all the time, but you're a gorgeous woman. I want you to sit next to me at dinner."

"I would be delighted to sit next to you."

"I see you don't have a drink. There is a bar at the back of this room. Would you like to go with me to get a drink?" He takes my arm, and we walk back toward the bar. It doesn't take me long to notice that he isn't looking at my face. I decide to pull his arm closer to my side so he can feel my breast with his arm as we walk back to the bar.

We each have a glass of champagne and take it over to where we are going to sit at dinner. There is a place card that doesn't have my name on it. He takes it, and hands it to the waiter, telling him to find another place for this person.

We sit and talk with each other, I turn to him, and when he is looking in my eyes, I do my 45-degree move, pretending to pick up my napkin. I see his eyes widen when he gets a good look at my assets. Occasionally, when we are talking, I place my hand on his knee and gently squeeze it.

Dinner is being served, and I can tell that some of the other women at the table are not happy with me. The table is a series of tables in a square. Where I am sitting in the middle of one section, I see Jim directly across from me at the far end.

I occasionally turn to him to see what his reaction is to what I am doing with Vito. He seems very pleased. I finally say to Vito, "I'm hungry."

Each of us turn to the table and begin our meal, and I continue the playful small talk. As they are serving dessert, Jim comes around the table, leans over, and speaks in Vito's ear: "We have a little bit of business to conduct. Perhaps we can go to the bar."

Vito gets up and says to me, "After I'm done with my business, I'll be right back."

The two men are right behind me, so I can't see what is going on. Suddenly, all hell breaks loose. At least two dozen men with guns come bursting into the room, holding up badges and saying, "FBI, nobody move. Put your hands in the air."

FBI agents go around the room handcuffing people, checking them for weapons and then leading them out of the room. Vito and Jim are in handcuffs, and an agent is carrying Jim's suitcase. All the women are allowed to retrieve their coats and then handcuffed and led out, including me.

Jim is in a different police wagon than I am in, and we are all taken to the same police station. Vito and Jim are booked first, and Vito is led off to jail while Jim is put in a holding room. The rest of the party attendees are also booked, and all the women and some of the men are released. I was booked but put in the same room as Jim. An officer comes in, takes off our handcuffs, and says we are free to go.

Life Lessons Learned:

Sometimes we get involved in situations where the adrenaline rush is unbelievable. We do things we never thought we could. In a moment that's full of excitement and suspense, we feel like we can do almost anything. Later, we have a more sober recollection of how much risk we were really taking, and we wonder if it was worth it to risk our lives for a thrill.

Some people have the uncanny ability to assess the risk in something quickly and decide to proceed and become heroes. There are many people in our lives who are heroes. We don't always know it. Heroes are people who try and make a difference. Look around where you work and where you live, even in your own family, and see if you can identify the heroes.

CHAPTER 68:

Hello, Mabel

I look at my watch when Jim leaves, and it is around midnight. It is 9 o'clock in San Diego, and hopefully Mabel will still be up.

I call, and she picks up on the third ring.

"Mabel, it's Red."

"Red, how are you? It's been a long time since we talked. Are you okay?"

"I just had the most exciting evening in my life." I tell her everything.

"I can't believe what happened. You helped the FBI arrest a weapons smuggler?"

"Yes, but after that, I broke up with my boyfriend and am ready to move to California."

"Are you kidding me? Do you want to come out here? When? How soon? I can't wait to see you."

"The first thing I have to do is check with the hospital to find out how much time I have left on my requirements for them to pay for my bachelor's degree."

"You got the bachelor's degree in nursing administration?"

"Yes, and I'm working at the hospital as a senior nurse, managing the nursing schedule and helping to teach new nurses."

"Are you still working in the ER?"

"Yes, that is where I manage nurses, and I love it. What do you think the possibility is of me getting a job in your hospital?"

"I don't know, but tomorrow I will find out and let you know."

"The sooner I can leave cold, dreary Chicago, the better. Tell me about the hospital and your life in San Diego."

"The hospital is huge; I think it is the biggest in the city. The people are very friendly, both doctors and nurses, and the lifestyle differs from Chicago."

"What do you mean when you say the lifestyle is different?"

"Chicago is very fast, everybody moves fast, and more exciting things are happening in Chicago. San Diego and the whole West Coast have a much slower pace. People aren't rushing to go anywhere or do anything. They take their time and enjoy the day. I live in a two-bedroom apartment. I had a roommate, but she left, and I have not replaced her. You have a place to come live immediately. I think you'll enjoy San Diego. The nightlife is different from Chicago, but there is nightlife. There are a lot of men. The weather, oh my God, the weather is unbelievable. When I came here, I brought all my winter clothes. Eventually, I got rid of all of them. I never want to wear them again. I often go to the beach, sit in a lounge chair, and enjoy the sun and the sea."

"It sounds amazing."

"Red, it is amazing. It's a growing city, and I think you will fit in better here than any other place you could go."

"Mabel, this long-distance call costs me a lot of money, but it's been worth it. Should we talk again tomorrow night and see what we discovered?"

"Are you kidding? Absolutely. I'm counting the hours!"

I hang up. I sit in my chair on a new high. I am experiencing the joy of knowing I can go to California and have a place to live while looking for work. I would live with the woman with whom I have shared many secrets. She has always been and will always be my best friend.

What an incredible day! What an impossible roller coaster ride, up and down. It took me a while to settle down to go to sleep. I had difficulty letting go of my memory of the white dress and working with the FBI to bring down a weapons smuggler. In my mind, I have a picture of a woman in that white dress with a magnificent body at a 45-degree tilt exposing just enough of her breasts to control a man. But it wasn't me, and my vision is fading rapidly as I fall asleep.

I get up the following day, put on my uniform, and get ready to go to work. During lunch, I go to the hospital administration department to determine how much time is left on my education reimbursement agreement. The person goes over to the file cabinet and finds my file. She says, "According to the records, you are obligated until the end of June 1937."

I think about it momentarily, then ask, "Is it possible to pay off the commitment? What would it be at the end of March 1937?"

She responds, "It looks like about $2,100."

"If I continue to work through the end of June, it will all be paid off. Is that correct?"

"Yes, it is."

I say, "Thank you. I'll let you know."

I keep my bankbook in my purse, and when I look, I see I have a balance of $1,500. I am going to get a payment from the FBI of $150. I would need money to go to California and probably buy some new clothes, although my uniform would work just as well in California's hospital as in a Chicago hospital. As much as I want to go immediately, the reality is that I can't afford it. I could ask my father for the money, but I won't because I still need more money to pay for my transportation and living expenses. If I wait and finish out my commitment here, I should have several thousand dollars in my bank account.

As promised last evening, I call Mabel and tell her what I found out and that I think it is possible to leave after the end of June. She tells me that she talked to the employment office, and they don't have an openings for a nurse manager, but they are always looking for licensed nurses to work in the hospital.

"It looks like you'll have a place to live and a job starting probably within a week when you get here. Do you realize I will have difficulty sleeping until you get here? I'm so excited about us being back together again."

I say, "Me too."

Life Lessons Learned:

True friends never leave you. They can go on a separate journey, but if you are true friends, you won't leave either. You may be separated for some time, perhaps even decades, but you're in each other's thoughts and memories regularly whether you talk or not, whether you exchange letters or Christmas cards or not. There are very few opportunities in life to make a true friend. You can tell if somebody is a true friend because, if you haven't talked to each other for a long time, when you do talk again, you pick up right where you left off no matter how long it has been.

I have never figured it out, but women are better at creating friendships than men. The exception may be soldiers, especially soldiers who go to basic training and war together. Over the course of my life as a nurse, I learned to understand more about the Band of Brothers in the military and just how special it is. I knew I could go to California and have a place to live while I was looking for work. I would live with the woman with whom I shared much. She would always be my best friend.

CHAPTER 69:

California, Here I Come

I decide to leave Chicago and move to San Diego. In the three months before I depart, Mabel and I run up large telephone charges. She finds me a job. I fill out an application and do a telephone interview with the head of personnel. I am given a temporary offer subject to an in-person interview when I get to California.

I return to Waterloo in early May to be with my mother on Mother's Day. I tell my parents that I am moving to San Diego. I didn't tell them about my adventures with the FBI. My parents are sad that I am leaving, but they understand I must follow my own path. I tell them that I will try and come back and visit them.

"It is a long trip from San Diego to Waterloo," I say. "Maybe you could come and see me in Southern California. I think the best time would be when it's winter in Waterloo."

They both chuckle and say they will think about it.

It is harder than I thought it would be to leave my friends at the hospitals, both doctors and nurses. We have had some fascinating cases and some challenging ones; all were great experiences, but I am ready for new experiences, and at the same time, I am a little nervous. I have two suitcases full of most of what I need. I have enough money to have my own sleeping compartment on the train.

The train is my home for two nights and three days. It is a totally different ride than the one from Waterloo to Chicago. I look out my window and see how flat the prairies are. I can see the destruction from the drought. The winds are blowing away the topsoil because it is so dry.

We go through a lot of little towns. I see a lot of people out of work. We pass thousands of closed shops and even more houses for sale. The first part of my journey helps me understand why they call it the Great Depression. I have a job, but I am feeling down. I am sick of what I see out the windows. People's lives fade away because of a lack of work.

The train travels for hours. The land is flat for hundreds and hundreds of miles. But then, suddenly, things start to change. I can feel the train climbing. The engine pulls a little more. It works harder to move the load. The train keeps going higher and higher.

The conductor tells us we are a mile up in the air in Denver. We continue and come face-to-face with the Rocky Mountains. We cross the peek, which it is over 12,000 feet. There are no towns, no shanties with people out of work. I see blue skies, rough mountains, and some snow leftover from the winter. Once we cross the top of the Rockies, the train uses very little power. The decline provides momentum for the train to move. I can feel the engineer pulling on the brake, trying to slow down the train's speed as it goes down toward ground level again.

The ride takes from Monday morning at 8 a.m. to 4 p.m. Wednesday when we arrive in San Diego. I am still on the train, as it is working its way through the train station. I get off the train, go to the baggage claim, and I think somebody is calling me. I can't tell for sure where it is coming from, but it is getting louder.

I finally can make out the word that is being cried out: "RED!"

When I understand the name, I know she is calling. I know it must be Mabel. Sure enough, she comes rushing to me, putting her arms around me. She kisses me, and I squeeze her as hard as she squeezes me.

We let go, step back, and look at each other. Happy with what we see, we decide it's time to go to Mabel's apartment.

We take a cab from Union Station to her apartment. The trip is about 25 minutes. I am taking everything in as Mabel points out important landmarks in the city. For the first time in my life, I see palm trees. The palm trees are everywhere. The colors of the houses are different from Chicago or Waterloo. They are bright and cheery. The colors are pastels, blues and oranges, and yellows and greens. The colors of houses in Chicago and Waterloo are strong white, blue, green, and gray. I fall in love with San Diego. The weather is beautiful, and the houses are beautiful.

We make a turn, and I can see the Pacific Ocean. I've never seen an ocean before. Mabel asks the cab driver to pull over, and we leave the cab to look at the ocean. Mable looks for a walkway, finds one, and we walk down to the beach and put our feet in the ocean.

We get back in the cab and finally wind our way up to her apartment. I pay the driver and gather my suitcases. We walk up the steps to a different kind of front door. It is round at the top, has a small window in the middle, and an iron grate over the window. When she opens the door, the wind blows out the front door into our faces.

I say, "Well, that's a strong wind."

Mabel says, "No, that's an ocean breeze. It can be quite strong at times. We have a breeze almost every day."

I am in love with my new home. I don't think I will ever want to leave this heaven on earth.

Life Lessons Learned:

Some people travel to get from one point to another, while other people take in the sites and the scenery and grow from the experience. I wanted the experience of a big city. I didn't want to stay in the small town of Waterloo, Iowa. When I got to Chicago, it was everything I hoped it would be. I had friends, places to go, things to see, and things to do.

The Depression caused many people to move who didn't want to but had no choice. What an incredible luxury if you can move because you want to. You can move because there's an opportunity to better yourself. The risk in moving is that you may not like where you wind up, and it may be challenging to return, but it was a wonderful challenge for me.

Prologue

My life has changed. I'm going to California to see what challenges and opportunities it presents. I'm both nervous and, at the same time, excited about what lies before me.